MC VINTAGE

The Seacastle Mysteries

Book 5

PJ Skinner

ISBN 978-1-913224-49-3

Parkin Press
INDEPENDENT PUBLISHER

Cover design by Mariah Sinclair

Discover other titles by PJ Skinner

The Seacastle Mysteries

Deadly Return (Book 1)

Eternal Forest (Book 2)

Fatal Tribute (Book 3)

Toxic Vows (Book 4)

Last Orders (Book 6 pending)

Mortal Mission: A Murder mystery on Mars

Written as Pip Skinner

The Green Family Saga (written as Kate Foley)

Rebel Green (Book 1)

Africa Green (Book 2)

Fighting Green (Book 3)

The Sam Harris Adventure Series

Fool's Gold (Book 1)

Hitler's Finger (Book 2)

The Star of Simbako (Book 3)

The Pink Elephants (Book 4)

The Bonita Protocol (Book 5)

Digging Deeper (Book 6)

Concrete Jungle (Book 7)

Also available as box sets on Amazon and AI narrated audiobooks on other retailers

Go to the PJ Skinner website for more info and to purchase paperbacks directly from the author: https://www.pjskinner.com

Discover other titles by PJ Skinner

The Seacastle Mysteries

Deadly Return (Book 1)

Eternal Forest (Book 2)

Fatal Tribute (Book 3)

Toxic Vows (Book 4)

Last Orders (Book 6 pending)

Mortal Mission: A Murder mystery on Mars

Written as Pip Skinner

The Green Family Saga (written as Kate Foley)

Rebel Green (Book 1)

Africa Green (Book 2)

Fighting Green (Book 3)

The Sam Harris Adventure Series

Fool's Gold (Book 1)

Hitler's Finger (Book 2)

The Star of Simbako (Book 3)

The Pink Elephants (Book 4)

The Bonita Protocol (Book 5)

Digging Deeper (Book 6)

Concrete Jungle (Book 7)

Also available as box sets on Amazon and AI narrated
audiobooks on other retailers

Go to the PJ Skinner website for more info and to
purchase paperbacks directly from the author:
https://www.pjskinner.com

felt a pleasant sugar rush energise me as I gulped down the rest of my coffee. The sun had emerged from behind the clouds warming the window nook overlooking the High Street. A painted lady butterfly bumped into the window panes trying to escape, but I did not let her out as I knew she would die. Instead, I mixed a pinch of sugar into a teaspoon of water and balanced it on the window frame, hoping she would find it whilst blundering about.

I opened a box at the back of the shop and removed some sixties era lampshades from its dusty interior. They were old stock from a shop in the East End, rescued by Harry's cousin Tommy. Unfortunately, I didn't receive them in time for Christmas, but I planned to design a kooky sixties window display with them for the Easter season. I remembered seeing a stuffed rabbit at the back of the shop that might complete the job. Taxidermy had been wildly popular at one stage in the Victorian era, and we still found peculiar examples of people's desire to preserve their pets or hunting trophies. I had once unearthed a batch of stuffed fish which found a home in the Surfusion restaurant diagonal from Second Home on the High Street. The owners, Rohan and Kieron, were preparing for a grand opening at Easter having been delayed by the death of Kieron's father. They had semi-adopted my friend Ghita who mediated in their quarrels and did their accounts and chivvied them into action when she was not making delicious cakes for the Vintage.

Time passed without me noticing as I soaped and cleaned the lampshades and laid them on newspaper to dry. The doorbell clanged, breaking through my concentration, and I wiped my hands on my apron as I headed for the front of the shop. To my surprise, Grace Wong stood in the doorway. Grace did not, as a rule, do social visits without being invited. She and Max were friendly and generous in our business dealings, but she had always seemed reticent about joining our friend group. Ghita had persuaded her to come along to several of her Fat Fighters exercise classes, which were an institution in Seacastle and an excuse to indulge in cake and gossip, but she exuded a mild air of disapproval at our frivolous attempts to keep fit.

'I expect it's cultural,' said Roz Murray, the town gossip. 'Hong Kong is a powerhouse of financial business. I don't expect there's much room there for messing around.'

'Chinese culture is about face and status,' said Joy, owner of the Shanty Pub, and (secret) secret agent.

Whatever concerned her, Grace glanced backwards as if she might bolt at any minute, her slight frame reminding me of a fawn on spindly legs.

'Are you busy?' she said.

'Not at all. Come upstairs and have a coffee.'

She nodded and followed me up the stairs to the Vintage. I debated closing the shop, but the High Street was almost deserted, so I left the sign on open. I made Grace a jasmine tea, her favourite, and cut her a sliver of cake. She always refused cake, but she often ate it, or wrapped it in a tissue to take for Max. She took a few sips of her tea while she composed herself. I didn't rush her and pretended to be sorting out the spoons.

'I'm so ashamed,' she said, breaking the silence. 'I don't know how to tell you what I've done.'

Her voice quavered. If it had been Ghita or Roz, I would have launched myself into encouragement or hugs, but I waited, knowing she would be uncomfortable with that. Finally, she looked up from her tea.

'It's the annual antiques fair. The woman who runs it.'

Unbidden, an image of Dorothy Parker-Styles loomed into my mind's eye like a tweed battleship.

'Dorothy?'

'Yes, her.'

Grace's skinny fingers interlaced, and she swallowed. I thought she might run out of courage, but she cleared her throat and pink spots of colour appeared on her cheeks.

'I've never got a table at the fair despite having a local business. We're supposed to have priority but…'

She tailed off. I had a moment of clarity. Dorothy had strong opinions about 'foreigners'.

'She doesn't pick you.'

'Well, this time, I, um, well, applied for a table in your name. No, that's not true. In your old name.'

My eyes widened.

'You did?'

'Well, she's such a snob, and she assumed that you're still married to George. The local DI's wife booking a table is a coup for her.'

I couldn't suppress a grin.

'Did she offer us a table?'

'In a prime spot.'

A ghost of a smile appeared on her lips.

'I'd call that a win. Are you going to take it?'

'You don't mind?'

'I owe you a favour, remember? If that silly woman wants to give me a table, let's take advantage of it. We can run it together. It'll be fun.'

'You're not annoyed?'

'Never look a gift horse in the mouth. Eat your cake and let's make a plan.'

Chapter 2

The front of the town hall had been constructed in the style of a Roman mausoleum with a pedimented gable end held up by Corinthian columns. The resulting portico contained the large, carved oak doors leading to the inner hall used for fairs and conferences since Victorian times. At the other end of the hall, a separate storage area had designated zones for each stall holder to keep their stock. Flimsy partitions stood between the zones, removing the temptation to cheat and creep across the painted boundaries. Fluorescent strip lighting flickered among the beams, giving the area a ghostly air.

The entry to the storage area was far more prosaic than the front entrance, having a pair of double doors made from pine and painted black, set in a wall made from concrete blocks. Outside the back doors lurked a shabby car park with cracked tarmac and faded paint dividers. Here the stall holders parked and unloaded their vans and lorries onto trolleys, queuing patiently until one became available. Acquaintances were renewed and friendships revived as stall holders trawled back and forwards through the doors and stacked their boxes and larger items in their allocated storage spot.

Grace and I pulled into a recently vacated space at the far end of the lot. I went to borrow a trolley while Grace positioned our vehicle with its boot facing into the access route and waited for Max. He appeared soon afterwards, riding his bicycle with neat precision, and locking it to a lamppost near the van. I turned back to watch him bounce over to her with a big grin on his face and his back fringe flopping over his face. Grace's eyes lit up and her stern expression dropped for an instant. I always wondered how on earth they got together. Chalk and cheese didn't quite capture it. Entering the storage area, I managed to snaffle one of the larger four-wheeled trolleys, but I soon found out why someone had abandoned it, as it pulled to the left like a dog after a squirrel. I wheeled it down the ramp with some difficulty, shrugging at Grace as she watched me struggle to align the wheels and approach the van in a straight line.

'Almost better than nothing,' said Max, taking a deep drag on his cigarette, but not lifting a finger to help me.

'You're welcome to try finding another,' I said.

'It will do,' said Grace. 'If Max doesn't like it, he can carry the boxes and we'll watch.'

'Whoa, I'll behave from now on,' said Max. 'I see I'm outnumbered.'

He stubbed out his cigarette with a flourish, and we set about unloading the van. I had contributed a couple of the best pieces from my shop, but most of the goods were from Grace and Max's emporium. Her exquisite taste shone out from everything she had picked to sell at the fair. I would have been glad to own any of them, but I knew I couldn't afford it. They bickered gently together as they loaded the trolley, but even without knowing them well, I could see their deep bond. I congratulated myself on agreeing to work with Grace. Maybe I would finally get to know them better. My happy thoughts were interrupted by a shout from across the car park.

'Oi, you! Dorothy double-barrelled shotgun, or whatever your name is. I want a word with you.'

The man who had shouted this had gone red in the face with ill-suppressed fury. He strode through the parked vans, bumping people out of his way, oblivious to the black looks he garnered, straight to where Dorothy Parker-Styles stood surveying the scene from the storage door. Even from a distance, I could see she represented a formidable challenge. A minor battle steamer in a tight wool suit with hair set into concrete curls; she stared out through tiny eyes in flaking mascara and pursed her lips. She placed plump hands with tight rings sunk into the flesh of her fingers on her ample hips.

The approaching storm did not appear to intimidate her in the slightest. In fact, she narrowed her eyes in a way that suggested pistols at dawn. We watched transfixed, with all the other dealers, mouths open, as he approached her. I thought I saw his shoulders droop a little as he realised that she had not backed down.

'Mr Loveday, isn't it?' she said, folding her arms.

She looked down at him through the reading glasses perched on the end of her thin nose.

'Roy Loveday. You know exactly who I am, you stuck up old bag. And you know exactly what's wrong too.'

'Maybe you'd like to tell me.'

'You gave my table away to some random woman. I've had the table every year since my mother died. I inherited it.'

Dorothy rolled her eyes.

'You can't inherit a table. Your mother had taste. The stuff you bring to the fair is fit for the junk yard, and lowered the whole tone of the event. I told you last year to step up or lose out. Well, now you have.'

The man's gaze fell on us and our rickety cart. He stared at Max and Grace, and a sneer creased his lips.

'Don't tell me you gave it to foreigners?' he said. 'They're taking over the country. I can't believe it.'

I stepped forward, giving him my best intimidating glare.

'My name is Tanya Bowe and my husband is the local D.I.,' I said, before a startled Grace could speak. 'I run a high-end antique shop here in Seacastle. I have just as much right as you to get a table. By the way, my friends are British, so you might like to apologise.'

Roy Loveday's thin, wiry frame quivered with rage

'You'll regret this,' he said, turning to Dorothy. 'I won't take it lying down. You've ruled the roost here for far too long. It's time you were replaced.'

He hawked and spat a gob of mucus on the ground at her feet. To give Dorothy her due, she didn't even flinch.

'We'll see about that, won't we?' she said. 'Empty threats won't get you any nearer to a table on my watch.'

'Who said they were empty?' said Loveday and stalked off towards the exit of the car park under the startled gaze of the other dealers. Max had gone quite white with fury, but Grace had grabbed his sleeve to prevent him following Loveday out onto the street.

'Nasty fellow. It's about time we got rid of him.,' said Dorothy, who seemed oblivious to Loveday's threats. 'I can't say I blame him, though. Who are you?' She looked pointedly at Grace and Max before ignoring them.

'I'm Tanya Bo-Carter, wife of D.I. George Carter of the Worthing Police.'

'George's wife? I'm surprised you need to lower yourself to such an event. D.I. Carter must be a tolerant man. Maybe we could get him to arrest Mr Loveday and save us all a world of trouble?' she said. 'If you follow me, I'll show you the table I allocated to you.'

I felt a rush of rage at her treatment of Grace and Max, but I didn't allow myself to speak. We wouldn't see her much during the fair and it would be up to Grace to decide whether to carry on after this first year. Maybe Dorothy would warm to her. We persuaded the trolley up the ramp and parked it in the storage space Dorothy indicated to us. Grace followed her into the main hall, forgetting for a minute she had pretended I would be the office stall holder. I hissed at her and she slowed to let me over take her. Dorothy steamed through the alley between the tables like a cargo ship down the Panama Canal, taking no prisoners. She did not bother to return greetings or smile at anyone. I could see why she raised people's hackles, and Roy Lovelace was not alone in resenting her.

'This is yours,' she said, gesticulating at a battered table in the middle of the row nearest the outer wall of the hall not a prime spot, but not the worst either.

A skinny young woman who resembled a scrawny chicken, wearing a Laura Ashley dress several sized too large for her, approached Dorothy carrying a cup of coffee. She took it from her without thanks and tested it for flavour. She glared and hissed at her.

'It's got sugar in it. How many times must I tell you not to put sugar in my coffee? Are you actually stupid, Abigail?'

The young woman blanched and shrank from her like a beaten stray.

'You had sugar yesterday,' she said. 'I'm sure…'

Dorothy thrust out her hand with the cup of coffee in it.

'Change it. Now.'

She slunk away, and Dorothy turned to face us again.

'Your table should be set up for the doors to open at ten o'clock sharp on Saturday, and cleared away by six o'clock on Sunday when the hall will be locked. I expect your accounts by Monday evening and ten per cent of your sales.'

'Ten per cent?' said Grace. 'We already paid two hundred pounds for the table.'

Dorothy raised an eyebrow and stared pointedly at Grace.

'I thought Mrs Carter paid the bills.'

'Oh, I do,' I said. 'Don't mind Grace. She's not good at numbers.'

Mrs Carter? It's been a long time since anyone called me that. George would have a fit if he caught me masquerading as his wife, especially as he is now an item with my sister, Helen. (Don't ask. It's a long story). Dorothy shook her head.

'I don't let foreigners have tables in my fair. Nelly Loveday would turn in her grave,' she said, and stomped off.

Grace looked as if she might explode with fury, but she swallowed and returned to organising the table.

'It doesn't do to get on the wrong side of Dot the Despot,' said the plump lady on the stall beside us. 'Her bark is not worse than her bite.'

'I'll bear that in mind,' I said. 'Who's the young woman?'

'That's her niece, Abigail. Poor lamb. Imagine being stuck with Dot as a guardian.'

'What happened to her parents?'

'Her mother died in a car crash when Abigail was three years old. Dot had to step in as the only relative. She's resented it ever since.'

Grace, who had waited for Dorothy to leave before speaking again, looked as if she would burst with indignation.

'This fair had better be worth it,' she said. 'What happens to the extra ten per cent?'

'What do you think?' our neighbour said, slapping her pocket. 'If you want to be a member of Parker's Posse, you have to pay your dues. By the way, I'm Veronica Higgins, and the fellow dragging in the stock is my long-suffering husband, Sid. We trade military stuff, like guns and knives and so on. The couple on the other side of your table are Rowan and Susie Parsons. They mostly sell prints and paintings.'

'I'm Tanya, and this is Grace. Her husband Max is doing the box carrying. They own the Antique Emporium on Seacastle High Street.'

'I've seen it. They always have such lovely window displays, but I don't go in. It's out of my league price-wise.'

'Have you been doing this for long?' I asked.

She chortled.

'Long enough. Luckily, most of the fairs we participate in are run by less unpleasant people. Dot is a real piece of work. You'll see.'

Chapter 3

It took us a few hours to set up the table and display shelves to Grace's satisfaction. While I despaired of her perfectionism, I had to admit that our table outshone the surrounding stalls by quite some margin. Max had left to run the Emporium as soon as Grace fussed about placing her stock and I couldn't do much other than lift and carry when required. Veronica had watched us closely, and she had not been fooled by my feeble attempts to direct operations.

'It's not your table, is it?' she said to me. 'I don't blame Grace for pretending. Our Dot isn't keen on immigrants. She would never have agreed to give Grace a table if she had known.'

'You won't tell her, will you? Grace has tried for years to get into the fair.'

'Of course not, ducks. Grace is a true professional. Her stall looks wonderful. Is she Chinese?'

Grace spun around, her eyes blazing with fury.

'I'm from Hong Kong. We are not Chinese. We are British.'

'I meant nothing by it, lovey. It's none of my business, only some stallholders here are funny about immigrants taking their business.'

'Like Roy Loveday, for instance?' I asked.

'Him, and there are others. You want to watch your stock,' said Veronica, pulling a cloth over hers. 'I'm off to get more bits and pieces. I'll see you later.'

Grace watched her go with ill-concealed disdain. I tried to distract her by pouring us a cup of tea from my flask. As I searched for something to say, I watched a flamboyant pixie of a man, dressed in a tight plum coloured suit with a multicoloured cravat, mince up to the Higgins' table and pick up several of their wares. Grace elbowed me and I turned to give her a smirk. The man came towards our table. He cocked his head first to one side and then the other.

'Oh my,' he said, stroking his goatee. 'We have an artiste in our midst. You can't be from around here with your exquisite taste.'

'I'm afraid I can't take the credit,' I said.

'I never thought you could, dearie,' he said. 'Introduce me to your elegant friend please.'

'I'm Tanya, and this is Grace. And you are?'

'Miles Quirk. Quirk by name, quirky by nature,' he said, extending a beautifully manicured hand towards Grace. 'Your stall is dreamy. I…'

His eyes popped open, and he reached for a little plate Grace had placed on a shelf.

'Oh, my word,' he said. 'I can't believe it.'

To my surprise, a single tear escaped from his eye and rampaged down his powdered cheek. Grace smiled.

'A Bawo and Dotter Limoges Art Nouveau Floral plate,' she said. 'It's very rare to find one on its own. People bought the complete set and passed it down to their children. I—'

'I'm so excited,' he said, without waiting for her to finish. 'You can't imagine how I've searched. I've been collecting my set for ten years and this will complete it. How much is it?'

'It's not for sale.'

I might have gasped. Miles Quirk's jaw dropped, and I thought he might faint with disappointment. He struggled to speak. Then Grace laughed.

'I'm sorry. I couldn't resist it. Of course you can have it. I'm afraid it's not cheap, though.'

He beamed.

'How much?'

'Fifty pounds.'

'I'll take it. Will you keep it for me?' he said. 'Only I'm off to a meeting and I can't take it right now. I'll bring you cash.'

'No problem. It will be here when you come back. I'll put a sold sticker on it.'

Suddenly, Dorothy Parker-Styles loomed over us, followed by her niece. Abigail's eyes opened as wide as saucers when she saw the plate in Miles's hand.

'Oh my goodness,' she said. 'You found the last piece. How amazing!'

Dot tried to grab it from Miles's hand, but he gave it to Abigail who examined it in awe. She turned it over and examined the markings on the bottom. A malevolent expression crossed Dot's face. She bumped Abigail's arm hard. I tried and failed to catch the plate as she dropped it on the floor where it smashed into smithereens. Dot glanced at the pieces with smug satisfaction. Miles Quirk staggered backwards and sat down hard on a plastic chair; the look of horror on his face replaced by one of hate and loathing.

'Clumsy girl,' said Dot to Abigail. 'That's just typical of you.'

Abigail bit her lip; 'You knocked it out of my hand,' she said, her voice shaking.

'I beg your pardon. I did no such thing.'

'But—'

'Honestly, I don't know why I bother,' said Dot to Grace, who had her mouth open in shock. 'I'll take it off your bill.'

She turned to leave. White-faced with fury, Miles stood up and shouted after her.

'You old witch,' he said. 'You knew how much I wanted that plate. How could you?'

'Don't shout at me. Abigail dropped it, not me. Control yourself or I'll throw you out of the fair.'

'Throw me out? I quit. And it's time we got rid of you too. You'll see. Your time is up.'

Dot rolled her eyes.

'I'd like to see you try,' she said.

She moved off under the scrutiny of the other stall holders who stood in front of their precious stock, protecting it from another accident. As soon as she had left the hall, an indistinct murmur broke out, which rose to a crescendo as people discussed the incident. I struggled to comprehend the scene I had just witnessed. Grace had gone white with shock and Abigail wept into a tissue.

'I'm so sorry, Miles,' said Abigail. 'I swear she made me drop it on purpose.'

'That's alright, sweet pea. I saw what happened. She couldn't bear me to be happy. She's a nasty, vindictive, old hag. Nothing like her sainted sister, God rest her soul.'

Abigail sniffed and dabbed at her eyes with a ragged tissue. Grace rummaged in her handbag and found her a clean one. Miles glanced at his watch and a look of alarm crossed his face.

'I can't be late for this meeting. I'm sorry about your plate, Grace. Keep an eye out for another one. I'm apparently still in the market.'

He walked off, picking his way past the benches, straining to keep his eyes off the myriad of goodies tempting him to stop. Grace leaned over to Abigail and lifted a fat curl off her face.

'Don't worry,' she whispered. 'I have a second one in the shop. He interrupted me when I was about to tell him. You can surprise Miles with it when he gets back.'

'Really? That would be wonderful.'

Abigail's face lit up, and I noticed her blue eyes shining like forget-me-nots planted on her skinny face.

'It may take me a while to find it in the storeroom at the shop, but I promise to bring it to you when I do,' said Grace.

'I'm sorry, but I didn't get your names. My aunt forgets to introduce me.'

'I'm Grace Wong and this is Tanya Bowe. The handsome man who is carrying our boxes is my husband, Max.'

'It's nice to meet you, Mrs Wong. And I apologise for my aunt. She's stuck back in colonial times, I'm afraid. It's so embarrassing.'

'I'm used to it. And it will be a pleasure to see her face when Miles completes his set.'

'Um, I've got to go now. She'll be expecting me.'

'See you later. And call me Grace.'

Abigail hurried after her aunt, bumping into one stall and almost knocking it over. Luckily, it contained nothing breakable.

'Let's hope that's the last of the dramas,' said Grace.

'I've a feeling they've just begun.'

Chapter 4

The sunny Saturday of the Seacastle Vintage and Antique Fair drew people out of their houses for the first time in days. A long queue of customers snaked down the pavement outside the hall, jostling for position. The owners of a local coffee van had parked near the hall and they did a brisk business selling coffee and doughnuts to those waiting in the queue. The rich aroma of freshly brewed coffee crept into the hall enticing the stall holders out onto the street to pick up a cup and a bite. Anticipation twisted my stomach into knots, as if I was about to play football for England, not run a stall at an antique fair.

People streamed into the hall as fast as Abigail could take their money. A few complained about the entry fee, but most paid up without a quibble. Grace's table was an instant hit, and I soon relaxed into the banter of the bargain with eager clients. I loved to watch someone pouch a treasure after a protracted negotiation. They tried to hide their triumph out of politeness, but I never let them know they had paid what Grace had wanted.

Soon Grace had to go to the storage area to select more goods for the table, leaving me to fend for myself. A smartly dressed man stopped to examine one of my pieces, an Alvar Aalto L-leg table that Harry and I had found in a house clearance the year before. Usually, I passed high value items on to Grace and Max, but Aalto's designs, though saleable, didn't count as antique and the prices frightened the people who came to Second Home looking for a bargain. Despite constant polishing, the table had languished unnoticed. The man flipped the table over, almost taking a lady's eye out. She pushed past him, muttering under her breath. He wrinkled his brow as he scrutinised the joints.

'It's fake, of course,' he said, picking at the label.

'Please don't do that,' I said. 'The table is original and so's the label. If you take it off, you must buy the table at full price.'

He sneered at me.

'That's naïve of you. I'm an expert and I can assure you it's a fake.'

My blood boiled, but I pretended to be crestfallen. I let my head drop.

'How did you know?' I asked.

'The name's Christie. Jasper Christie. You might recognise my surname.'

He lifted his chin in pride. What a poser! I doubted he belonged to the famous Christie's auction house family, but I didn't say so. I recognised the stolen line from James Bond. He handed me a business card with raised lettering and a gold crest on it. I pretended to consider it.

'I do. But that doesn't change the facts. The table has a known provenance. It's the genuine article.'

He sighed.

'I'll give you two hundred for it.'

'That wouldn't buy one leg. It's nine hundred and fifty pounds.'

'And where's my profit? What's your dealer-to-dealer price?'

I smirked.

'I couldn't sell you a fake table. I've got my reputation to think of.'

He stiffened and replaced it under the stall.

'You think you're so clever. You could've sold it right now instead of taking it home again. My next offer won't be so generous.'

'I'll take my chances.'

Christie strode off, pushing his way through a group of indignant punters. Susie Parsons, on the stall next door, shuffled across to poke me in the arm.

'Well done you,' she said. 'I heard it all. He's a conman. You don't want to believe a word he says. He always tries to intimidate fresh faces.'

'Thanks for the heads up. He was rather aggressive.'

'That's like saying the sea is rather wet,' said her husband, Rowan. 'You need to watch out for him. He doesn't like to lose out. I'd take the table home tonight if you don't sell it. Things have disappeared once he takes a fancy to them.'

'But how does he enter the hall?'

Susie tapped the side of her nose.

'They say he's got an arrangement with Dot the Despot. He provides services for access to the hall.'

'Services?'

She cackled in unison with her husband.

'Do I have to spell it out for you?' he said.

'Poor deluded Abigail holds a torch for the conman,' said Susie. 'But it's strictly business for him. He does nothing for free, and she only has her heart to offer him.'

'Talk about poor taste,' said Rowan, and they both sniggered.

'Poor Abigail. I heard she got stuck with Dorothy.'

'Dot. No one calls her Dorothy. Yes, Abigail's mother died when she was still a child. I have never heard her talk about a father,' said Susie.

'It seems Dot was left holding the baby,' said Rowan. 'Her parenting skills are non-existent, as you might imagine.'

'Did you know Abigail's mother?' I asked.

'I went to school with her. Felicity, that was her name. The nicest woman you ever met. Mind you, she always had a weird side.'

Before I could get her to elaborate, Grace returned from the storage area with a boxful of eclectic goods. Soon, eager customers clamoured around our table and the fair took over again. We were shattered by the time the last visitor had been ushered out. Grace stuffed the cash takings into her pocket. She had a card reader, which had also been in constant use. From her radiant expression, I gathered her day had been a success. I had not sold the Alvar Aalto table yet, but I had shifted a couple of kitchen stools and a lacquered box. Susie's advice about Jasper Christie had resonated with me, so I carted the Aalto table home. Grace also removed the best pieces from our table and shut them in a locked box in our storage area, which she chained to a bracket on the wall.

'That should stop even the most determined thief,' she said. 'I'll be here early tomorrow. I want to redesign the table with a primary colour theme.'

'That sounds fantastic. Can I bring a couple of my sixties lampshades? They will fit right in.'

'Of course. I'll see you then.'

As I left, I saw Jasper Christie exiting via a side door. A shiver went up my spine. Horrible man. I hoped Susie and Rowan had been exaggerating about his habits, but they had a ring of truth to them. I couldn't wait to get home to Mouse and Hades and snuggle on the sofa while we chatted to Harry on WhatsApp.

Chapter 5

The next day, a chilly mist hung over the town, swaddling the buildings in its damp embrace. I drove to the hall early, as I couldn't sleep, knowing Grace would be there working her magic on inanimate objects from the last century. I wondered if she had found another side plate for Miles Quirk. He had not returned to the fair after his meeting, and his table remained covered in a waxed tablecloth. Could he afford to lose the business? When I got there, Grace's car sat by itself in the back row of the car park and I pulled in alongside it. I felt the bonnet of her car—still warm despite the cold—and cradled the flask of jasmine tea I had brought with me.

The door to the storage area hung open, but the lights hadn't yet been switched on. I peered into the gloom and spotted Grace leaning over into one of the storage spaces. I guessed she had spotted something irresistible to purchase. Antique fairs are to dealers what libraries are to bookworms; leaving without acquiring a new heart's desire seemed impossible, even if you had only intended to get rid of some old ones. I approached with caution, not wanting to startle her, but I was the one who got startled. Dorothy Parker-Styles sat rigid in the storage cubicle; a look of utter astonishment carved into her features. An ornate knife handle protruded from her chest. This was no accident. I coughed to alert Grace to my presence. She turned her shocked face to me. I could see her hands trembling.

'It wasn't me,' she said. 'I found her like this.'

'Is she dead?'

'I presume so.'

'Don't touch her. Flo Barrington, the coroner, can determine the time of death from the body's rigidity. I'll make sure they bring her with them.'

Grace's face fell.

'Are you going to call the police?'

'Of course. What else would I do?'

'What if they arrest me? Can't we just go home and let someone else find the body?'

Her brow shone with cold sweat. I thought she might faint for a moment as she wobbled on her thin legs.

'Why would anyone arrest you?'

She didn't answer, shaking her head and backing away from the body.

'The police need to be told straight away,' I said. 'George will come with Flo to examine the scene, followed by the scene of crime officers. Time is of the essence if they want to find out who did this.'

I took out my phone and speed dialled George, waiting impatiently for him to answer. He had become even more punctilious since he had teamed up with my sister, Helen. He would not dream of answering the phone while he was driving. I could imagine him searching for a safe space to pull in as he listened to his phone ring. I hopped from foot to foot in my impatience.

'Come on, George. Answer the phone.'

I think he heard me. He tutted.

'Patience is a virtue, Tan. Your sister puts you to shame on that front.'

'I don't need a lecture right now. We have a body.'

I heard an intake of breath.

'Another one? For heaven's sake. I don't know how you do it.'

'I don't do anything. They follow me around like Jessica Fletcher. Someone is having a laugh at my expense.'

A further loud sigh on George's end of the line.

'Is anyone else there with you and the deceased?'

'Grace. She found the body. I…'

I looked around, but Grace had disappeared. I blinked twice to make sure I hadn't imagined the entire scene, but Dot still sat astounded in the storage cubicle.

'Tan? Are you still there?'

'Yes. Um, but Grace has gone. She seemed very shocked. Maybe she has gone outside for some air.'

'We'll find her. Where are you anyway?'

'I'm in the storage area behind the town hall.'

'Please don't budge from there. Can you put up some sort of cordon? We need to make sure no one approaches the body.'

'I'll try. Please hurry and bring Flo. I don't think this is a natural death.'

'And how would you know?'

'There's a knife sticking out of her rib cage.'

George swore.

'On my way. Hold tight.'

I put my phone back in my handbag and looked around for some sort of rope or tape. I was loath to root around in other people's storage spaces in case someone arrived and caught me in the act. Many implications could have been drawn, considering Dot's body was the only other person in the space. I locked the door into the hall, so nobody could get in from there, and then I tied a belt around the handle of the door to the car park so no one could enter without me helping them. Before I secured the door, I tried to spot Grace in the carpark, but her car had gone. I couldn't understand why she had left.

She had no motive to kill Dot, despite the woman's appalling rudeness. I had never seen Grace do anything hot blooded or spontaneous. She had the constitution of a lizard. And yet, I couldn't say I knew her at all. She joined in with our gatherings, but always on the fringes, and I often had the idea she disapproved of our frivolity.

I realised I still had the flask of jasmine tea with me, so I sat opposite Dot on a rather nice oak farmhouse chair and poured myself a cup. The hot liquid helped to calm my nerves and release the brain freeze that had affected me since I had arrived. I needed to give George some concise information about Dot and her potential killer, and it occurred to me there were several prime suspects in clear view. The problem for George would be the severe unpopularity of the woman. I couldn't recall anyone with a nice thing to say about her. It seemed she had swindled or insulted most people at the fair over her tenure. I wondered how Abigail would take Dot's demise. Despite their fraught relationship, I presumed she had some attachment to the woman who had brought her up. It would be a shock, no matter what.

I took out my Poirot notebook, as Harry called it, and my pen, and made some notes. Who had most to gain from Dot's death? Presumably, someone would take over the fair, but was that a motive to kill her? Roy Loveday and Miles Quirk had both threatened her, but they weren't the only one with grudges. Did Jasper Christie have a motive? I felt like he would do anything for money. Who had had access to the storage room after the fair closed for the night? There were too many suspects at first glance. But then I remembered the knife. I stood up and edged closer to the body, almost apologetic.

The knife had been buried into Dot's plump chest and blood had soaked into her floral dress. I presumed it had pooled beneath her or run under the boxes in the cubicle against which she had been propped up. I crouched down and examined the handle of the knife. Its intense black colour struck me as unusual and I could see some sort of inscription on the blade. The guard had an ornate design incorporating a serpent. Weapons were not my speciality, and I did not recognise the design as belonging to any era. The Higgins had an entire table of them, but I couldn't remember seeing this knife among them.

I slipped my phone out of my handbag and took a couple of quick photographs of the hilt. It wasn't until I stepped back again that I realised how macabre it was to photograph a knife still stuck in a victim. I went to delete the pictures from my phone, disgusted at myself. What could I have been thinking? A loud rattling interrupted me and alerted me to the arrival of some dealers. I shoved the mobile phone back into my handbag and approached the door. Loud voices protested about being locked out. I recognised Rowan Parson's Somerset burr among the indignant demands to be let in. I glimpsed his bald head through the gap.

'You can't come in, I'm afraid. There's been an incident.'

'There'll be a larger one if you don't open the door,' said a voice I didn't recognise.

I sighed. There would be no easy way to tell the dealers that their best earning fair of the winter would not be going ahead.

'Dorothy Parker-Styles is dead, and it looks like murder. The police are on their way to the hall.'

'What did she say?'

'She says Dot is dead.'

'Dead? Are you sure?'

I was certain, but I didn't reply.

'Serves her right. She had it coming,' said someone.

'You shouldn't speak ill of the dead.'

'And why not? She never said a kind thing about anyone her whole life. Miserable old hag.'

'What about our stock?'

'And the fair? Will it be cancelled?'

The question hung in the air. I had to answer it.

'I don't know,' I said. 'It seems likely, though.'

A chorus of disapproval greeted my reply making me glad I had blocked the door.

'Trust Dot to ruin everyone's day even in death,' said Veronica Higgins. 'Can't we at least get our stuff from the hall?'

The sound of a siren split the air and a squad car drove through the car park and forced people to move aside, stopping outside the door. I removed the belt from the handle and looked out. P.C. Joe Brennan left his vehicle, adjusting his hat as he turned to the crowd.

'Move away now. Nothing to see here.'

The grumbling reached a crescendo before someone knocked on the door.

'Tan? It's me. Open up.'

I released the latch. George and Flo came through the door dressed in their forensic suits. It always made me smirk to see him in a shower cap. Flo grinned at me.

'They should hire you to travel to areas with a low murder rate,' she said. 'You keep everyone on the force employed for months down here.'

'I'd make more than I earned at this fair anyway. It's a disaster for the dealers.'

'Where's the body?' said George.

'It's in that cubicle,' I said.

Flo shuffled over in her covered shoes and assessed the scene, looking for any vital signs from Dot who sat rigid like a large doll with her legs sticking out in front of her. Flo leant over to take Dot's pulse and turned to shake her head at George. The scene of crime officers had arrived, and Flo directed the photographer to video the scene before taking some close ups of the body.

'How long has the body been here?' said George.

'It's hard to say, but it appears to be in rigour. That makes the time of death at least a few hours ago, perhaps over six.'

'Has the body been moved?' said George.

'I don't think so. She may have been propped up here after being stabbed, or just fallen backwards and ended up like this. I'll know more when they remove the body for autopsy.'

'What about the knife?' I said. 'Do you recognise the type?'

'Some sort of dagger, judging by the hilt, but again, I'll know more when I remove it from the body.'

George coughed.

'And what's it got to do with you? I hope you will not interfere with my investigation. I'm not in the mood.'

I swallowed my reply. He had every right to get annoyed. I couldn't help myself. He would have exploded had he known about the photographs on my phone.

Abigail Nash came through the door from the hall. I hadn't realised she might have a key. In truth, I had almost forgotten about her existence. Her mousey character faded into the background. Now she looked flushed and had bed hair. She wore the same clothes as the day before. I wondered where she had been.

'What's going on?' she said. 'Don't tell me there's been another robbery. My aunt will go ballistic…'

She tailed off as she spotted Dot on the ground. Her eyeballs almost fell out of her head as she stared at her aunt in disbelief. Then she screamed, a high-pitched keening sound, eerie and odd. George motioned me to take her away. I didn't want to, but rather than irritate him further, I nodded and tried to take her arm. She shrank from my touch.

'Is she dead?' she said.

'I'm afraid so. But she didn't suffer,' I said, not sure if I was lying or not, wanting to save her feelings.

Abigail turned to look at her aunt, sitting in a pool of blood like a gory Barbie. She blinked a few times, and I waited for her to wail again. Then, to the shock of everyone in the room, she laughed, hands on her hips, shaking with mirth.

'The devil came for her at last,' she said, suddenly serious. 'Serves her right for killing my mother.'

Chapter 6

Given Abigail's reaction to her aunt's death, George took her to the station for questioning. When she had calmed down, I shepherded her over to a female P.C. who put an arm around her shoulders and steered her gently out of the door to a patrol car. I rolled my eyes when P.C. Brennan came over to me with his tablet and waved it in my face.

'We meet again,' he said. 'Would you care to elaborate on your presence at yet another murder scene? Is this some strange new internet craze I haven't heard of?'

I punched his arm, but not too hard. I didn't want to be charged for assaulting a police officer. He pretended to flinch and gave me a wry grin. He probably had a standing bet with the rest of the team on whether I would be involved every time they went to a murder scene. I couldn't believe it myself. Yet here I was again. Joe's questions were brief and to the point. He had applied to become a detective and had exams coming up. I felt sure he would pass. He had a methodical mind and tenacious character, both essential to the role.

When I had finished giving my statement, George beckoned me to one side.

'Look, I don't want you to get involved in my case, but I'd appreciate it if you'd have a word with Grace. She needs to come to the station and make a statement about finding the body. She seems like such a law-abiding lady and so refined compared to most of your women friends. I'm surprised she left the scene of a murder. Do you think it's a cultural thing?'

George's opinion of my friends was always a bone of contention between us. He considered Roz to be a flake, and to tell the truth, she suffered from exaggeration and a liking for extreme gossip. And he made fun of Ghita's exercise classes, calling us the fat fighters, instead of Fat Fighters. He had toned down his criticism a little since he went out with my sister Helen, but not much. Grace on the other hand, had always impressed him. Her cool exterior and high aesthetics gave her class in his eyes. George was a sucker for 'classy broads', as he called them. He and Harry often talked like gangsters together. They thought it sounded cool. And George was tone deaf when it came to culture. He had no idea how to deal with anyone who might be 'from abroad'. I sighed.

'I don't know, to tell you the truth. It might be something to do with her past life in Hong Kong. She's funny about the police. Do you remember when she got mugged at her shop by Wayne Dawson and didn't report it? Even though he took quite a large sum of money?'

'I'd forgotten, but you're right. She's not comfortable with the police. Maybe she's a member of a Triad?'

I guffawed.

'Don't be ridiculous. Grace is no more a member of a Triad than you are. She runs an antique emporium, not a nightclub.'

'What about her husband?'

'I don't know Max at all well.'

'Can you find out about him?'

'I thought you wanted me to stay off your case.'

'I do. But you know them better than me. They might tell you things without me having to force the issue. I don't want to upset them more than is necessary.'

'Fair enough. I'll do what I can. But first I have to find her.'

'Doesn't she live above the shop?'

'She does. I'll try there first.'

As I left, the waiting dealers surrounded me, clamouring for information. I pushed through them, giving no details of the case away. The rumour mill had already been churning, as was bound to happen, and Veronica Higgins appeared at my elbow, gurning with delight at the excitement.

'Did you see the body?' she said. 'Is she really dead?'

'As a doornail,' I said.

'Do they know who did it?'

'I'm sure they'll find out.'

'I have a few ideas,'

'Maybe you should speak to my ex-husband, D.I. George Carter. He'll be happy to take your statement, if you feel you know something important. I expect he'll want to talk to all of you.'

This set off a round of excited comments and competitive invention between the dealers who all imagined they knew more than their neighbours about who the suspect could be. I noticed Roy Loveday had reappeared. He smirked at me as I walked to my car, sending a shiver up my spine. What was he doing back at the fair? He had a grudge against Dot, which he had threatened to settle. I should text George from the car and let him know to send Joe Brennan out to question Roy before he disappeared.

I slipped away and got into the Mini, leaving the dealers milling around and exchanging theories. I felt sorry for them missing out on the fair, but they reminded me of a gathering of sharks around a dead whale. They showed Dot no mercy. She had made her deathbed and now she would have to lie in it. I had rarely come across someone with such a talent for rubbing people up the wrong way and being oblivious to the consequences.

Nobody noticed me leaving the car park as they had surrounded Joe Brennan to complain about being shut out of the storage area. I could just see his hat above the crowd as he attempted to field their questions. A few drops of rain landed on my windscreen, and soon a full-blown deluge fell on Seacastle. At least George and the lads would get some respite from the dealers who would invade the nearest café to get away from the rain. At least it guaranteed they would be easy to find until they dispersed again.

Even with the windscreen wipers at full speed, I could hardly see a thing as I crawled towards the High Street. I found a space in the Marks and Spencer car park and scrabbled around in the back of the car for my umbrella. The rain had diminished, but I dreaded going out without one. I found it in the footwell behind me and opened it out into the rain. I concentrated so hard on avoiding getting wet from above that I trod into a deep puddle at my feet. The freezing water soaked into my shoe which didn't improve my humour. What on earth was Grace playing at?

I scampered between the puddles, preserving my one dry foot. Walking through the food hall and the women's department of the store, I emerged onto the High Street and headed for the Asian Emporium. As usual, the window display created a magic kingdom with its eclectic and beautiful contents. Grace has used a well-worn rocking chair as the centrepiece and had draped a fabulous quilt over an Art Deco cocktail cabinet beside it. The interior of the shop was dark and the entrance door locked, which told me Grace had either left town or had hidden upstairs with Max.

I rang the doorbell at the side entrance and waited. When nobody came to the door, I texted Grace and then

Max, telling them I needed to speak to Grace and pleading for shelter from the rain, which had got heavier again. I heard the stairs creak, and the door opened a crack.

'Are you alone?' said Max.

'Yes, and I'm soaking wet. Can I come in before I get washed down the road?'

He held the door ajar, and I ducked under his arm, mounting the whinging stairs with some trepidation. After all, Grace had behaved as if I had caught her with her hand in the cookie jar. Could she have stuck a knife in Dot in a fit of fury and then repented? I entered their pristine sitting room, a veritable bomb of chinoiserie. Some parts of the Royal Pavilion in Brighton were the nearest thing I could compare to its miniature splendour. Grace huddled in a wide armchair which was covered in a red fabric decorated with golden dragons chasing each other around jagged mountains. Her pale face showed no emotion as I sat opposite her on a similar over-the-top chair in blue silk covered in blossoming cherry trees. Grace sniffed.

'I'm not good at hiding,' she said. 'I have nowhere to go.'

'But why did you leave at all?' I asked. 'I don't understand. You didn't kill her, did you?'

My face must have been a picture, because she snorted, and I saw her shoulders relax a little.

'I hope that's English humour. Of course I didn't. I would have used puffer fish poison and covered my tracks, not stabbed her in broad daylight.'

'Why don't I find that reassuring?'

'Come on. Don't you know me at all?'

I shook my head.

'Not really. Not like my other friends. You're...'

'Inscrutable?' she said, daring me to laugh at the racist trope.

'I was going to say private.'

She drew her knees up to her chest.

'That's true. Max and I like to keep to ourselves.'

Max, who had stayed standing, nodded. He crossed the room and scooped her onto his lap as if she weighed no more than Hades. He brushed some stray hairs from her face.

'It's not personal,' he said. 'We have trust issues. We had friends in Hong Kong who—'

Grace put her hand up to his mouth and shushed him. 'She doesn't need to know this.'

'Will it explain what happened at the hall?' I asked.

'Maybe,' said Max. 'What did you find there?'

'I don't know yet, but somebody stabbed the unpleasant manager of the fair and left her dead in a storage cubicle.'

'It wasn't me,' said Grace.

'I know that. The body had rigor mortis. It had been dead for at least six hours.'

'Oh. Do the police know?'

'Flo, you know her. She examined the body and told me. She needs to carry out an autopsy, but unless you were there since midnight, you won't be under suspicion.'

'She was here with me, in bed until seven in the morning,' said Max.

'You need to confirm that with the police,' I said. 'Please tell me what happened, Grace.'

Grace sighed.

'I found Dot's body when I entered the storage area. I went to that cubicle because I had spotted something interesting yesterday. and I wanted to check it out.'

'And you found the body?'

'Just as you came in. I panicked.'

'I'm not surprised after how she treated you.'

Grace sighed.

'I told you. I'm used to it.'

'But why are you afraid of the police?'

'That's my fault,' said Max. 'Would you like a tea? I'll tell you all about it.'

Chapter 7

Max waited until we all had steaming cups of tea before he cleared his throat to speak. He started in a halting fashion as if searching for the right words, but his English was as exquisite as their décor and far better than mine, so I put it down to nerves.

'What do you know about Hong Kong's history?' he asked.

'Less than I should,' I said. 'I remember the territory being handed back to China by Chris Patten in the nineties, after the lease ran out. And something about one country, two systems, but that's all I'm afraid.'

'It's more than most people know. Anyway, Hong Kong was first ceded to Britain in 1842 through the Treaty of Nanking after the first Opium War. In 1898, the two countries agreed on a ninety-nine-year lease for Britain, which led to a period where the Hong Kong economy thrived under laissez-faire polices and a skilled workforce. When the lease ran out in 1997, the British handed the territory back under certain conditions intended to protect Hong Kong's autonomy and way of life under Chinese sovereignty.'

'The agreement signed by Chris Patten?'

'Yes, that one. The one country; two systems formula specified that Hong Kong would keep its capitalist economic system and political freedoms for fifty years after the handover. Unfortunately, the Chinese undermined the agreement from the start. In 2003, hundreds of thousands of people marched against a bill which would have criminalised subversion against the Chinese government. The governor of Hong Kong tried and failed to introduce democratic elections to the territory. Tensions simmered as debates over democratic reforms and universal suffrage continued.'

'Did you and Grace get involved in the protests?'

'Not as such. Grace's family is from the top rung of society and were insulated from the effects of the changes. That shielded us for a good while despite me working for one of the few independent newspapers left in Hong Kong and covering the protests from Hong Kong's point of view. That brought me to the attention of the authorities, but they didn't have any legislation to stop me reporting the truth.'

'Weren't you scared?'

'Not scared enough. I had idealistic visions about a democratic Hong Kong which blinded me to the intentions of the Chinese government. With hindsight, a crackdown became inevitable once the protests became unmanageable. That happened in 2014, when the umbrella movement emerged as a protest against the Chinese government's pre-screening of candidates to elect Hong Kong's chief executive.'

'The umbrella protests? I remember them.'

'The protesters used umbrellas as passive resistance to protect themselves against pepper spray and tear gas. Despite continuing protests, the movement did not achieve its goals, which galvanised a new generation of activists. I followed these protests in my articles, but the government clamped down on the free press and banned my newspaper.'

'Is that when you left Hong Kong?'

'We hung on as long as possible, but when the government tried to introduce an extradition bill that would allow the transfer of convicted individuals to China, we knew our time was running out.'

'Then we found out the local police chief, who was supposed to be a friend of ours, had reported Max to the authorities. They were planning to arrest and try him for sedition against the Chinese government. We had to get out or go to prison,' said Grace.

'So, we withdrew all our cash and sold our flat for half its value before fleeing to Britain. We had a right to British citizenship thank goodness, or I don't know where we could have gone.'

'And ended up in Seacastle?'

'That's a long story,' said Max. 'Not one for today.'

'Is that why you don't trust the police?' I asked.

'I'm afraid they might deport us from Britain if I'm charged with murder. We would not survive imprisonment in China.'

'But you found a body already in rigor mortis. Nobody thinks you killed Dorothy. George has a huge amount of respect for you. He just needs your statements.'

'I'll take her to the station later,' said Max. 'Give us a couple of hours.'

'Okay, but don't kill anyone else, Grace. I won't be able to cover for you.'

Grace laughed despite her worries.

'I'll try not to,' she said.

After Max had promised to take Grace to the station, I walked back to the car and made notes about our chat. I felt sorry for them being ripped from the country of their birth and seeing it change without being able to save it. Everything is fine until it isn't. No wonder Grace didn't trust the police. I hoped George would go gently on her. I send him a text telling him they would drop by the station later and drove myself home.

Mouse raised his eyebrows as I stumbled through the front door, drenched and disgruntled. He put the kettle on without me asking and got me a clean hot towel from the airing cupboard.

'Did you have a fight?' he said.

'A fight? With who?'

'Grace. The fair can't be over yet. It's barely midday.'

'I didn't fight with Grace. The fair was cancelled.'

'Cancelled? You're joking. Why?'

'The usual.'

Mouse's eyes widened.

'You're joking, right?'

'No, I'm not; and don't look at me like that. I didn't do it.'

Mouse giggled.

'I think Jonah had a better reputation than you. What happened?'

'Somebody stabbed the manager of the fair and dumped her body in the storage area.'

'It's not Grace who's dead then?'

'Hilarious. Do you want to know about it or not?'

'I'm dying to hear all the gory details.'

I grimaced.

'It was quite gruesome. The dagger was still embedded between her ribs.'

'Oh, how gross. What sort of dagger was it?'

I remembered the photograph on my cell phone I had failed to delete and I felt a hot flush suffuse my cheeks.

'I don't know.'

'You've gone bright red. Are you sure you weren't involved?'

'Don't be ridiculous. Look, don't tell your father, but I took a photograph of the hilt. I meant to delete it, but things snowballed.'

'You have a photograph? You're a badass. Can I see it?'

'I suppose so. Maybe we can identify the type of dagger using an app.'

Mouse narrowed his eyes in faux disapproval.

'An app? Are you serious?'

'We might figure out who owned the dagger if we knew what type it was.'

'Did George tell you not to interfere with his case?'

'What do you think?'

'I think I need to see this photo.'

Chapter 8

Mouse could not pinpoint the purpose of the knife protruding from the ribcage of Dorothy Parker-Styles. According to Google, similar daggers, known as athames, were linked to witchcraft. I had never believed in new age magic and witchcraft, and threw my eyes to heaven when they were mentioned. I did not leap to any conclusions about the use of that dagger to kill Dot, presuming it was the first one that came to hand in a heated argument, rather than a targeted killing. Even my imagination couldn't stretch to envision Dot being killed by some sort of satanic cult.

I left him to research the stallholders who had clashed with Dot in our presence. No doubt there were more unhappy punters at the hall, but I stuck to the ones I felt had motive. In that list I included Rowan and Suzie Parsons, Veronica and Sid Higgins, Roy Loveday, Miles Quirk, Jasper Christie and Abigail Nash. None of them liked her and several had powerful reasons for having a heated row, which could have escalated into a stabbing. I had also given the same list to George. He had interviewed Grace, and he confessed to me she had become quite agitated while being questioned about Dot's racism.

'Do you think she's hiding something?' I asked.

'I don't know. She's rather hard to read. She could have stabbed Dot earlier and come back to hide the body. You may have disturbed her in the act.'

'Trust me. I'm as sure as I can be that she had nothing to do with it.'

'We don't work on your hunches. We follow the evidence. Flo will do an autopsy on the body in the next couple of days. We may find physical evidence on the body. Fibres and such like. I asked Grace to give us the clothes she was wearing, but she said she had washed them already. That's suspicious, don't you think?'

I didn't reply. Although Grace hadn't been on my list of suspects, he had raised a valid point. Her behaviour invited suspicion, even if it was down to her fastidious nature. I intended to do my own investigation and clear her as soon as I could. I didn't trust George to cover all the bases. He fixated on one suspect and try to fit his evidence around them rather than be led to the suspect by the evidence. Luckily, P.C. Joe Brennan, who had a more pragmatic view of a suspect's guilt, had become an invaluable part of the investigations team as he worked towards getting his detective sergeant's qualification. And I had a secret weapon. My sister Helen. George listened to her. All I had to do was to get her to listen to me, which was not as easy as it appeared.

News of the murder spread like wildfire around Seacastle, and as usual, it acted like catnip for my friends Roz and Ghita, who came straight to the Second Home in search of gossip. I had not long arrived at the shop when they came in carrying a litre of milk and Ghita's latest creation, a carrot and ginger cake with spiced orange frosting. I almost drooled at the description. Ghita's cakes were a massive success in the Vintage. People always went upstairs intending to only have a coffee, but her recipes were so tempting that many succumbed to saying things like 'I shouldn't really'.

'Wow, that looks amazing,' I said. 'I'll put up the cake of the week sign later. Customers will flood in to try it.'

'Can't we try it first?' said Roz.

I sighed.

'You're going to eat my profits.'

'Or my salary,' said Roz.

'Hm. Fair enough. I'll make the coffee. Do you have a date to open the Surfusion yet, Ghita?'

'I'm not sure. They've been snowed under with catering requests since George's wedding, and Kieron's mother's delicate state of health since the death of his father has necessitated constant visits to her. So, he is reluctant to commit to opening the restaurant until late spring.'

'What a saga. Poor old Rohan must be suffering. He just wants a quiet life,' said Roz.

'Unlikely, having Kieron as a partner. Ghita needs to do a WWF refereeing qualification to keep those two under control.'

'It's such a pity. The restaurant is beautiful now; the only thing left to do is open it,' said Ghita, tossing back her thick braid of dark brown hair and sighing.

She picked at the crumbs on her plate. Roz's brow furrowed, and she drummed her fingers on the table.

'Enough about Surfusion. Are you going to spill the beans on the murder or what?'

I smirked. I had been amazed at her self-control to this point, but her impatience had got the better of her. Why else would she have traipsed up to Second Home when her dishy husband Ed would sail into Pirate's Harbour at any minute? Only the juiciest piece of gossip would make her risk missing his arrival and their subsequent passionate reunion. They had been together for years, but their fiery temperaments kept their relationship on the boil. That and Ed's frequent absences on his fishing boat.

'I thought you'd never ask,' I said, grinning.

I described the lead up to the fair and Grace's subterfuge. I took my time relating Grace's visit to the shop to confess about it. Ghita didn't hide her amazement.

'Grace lied? I don't believe you. Grace is like an emissary of truth. She's holier than thou.'

'She's holier than the Pope,' said Roz, laughing at her own joke.

'It surprised me, I can tell you. Anyway, when we got to the fair to organise Grace's table, we witnessed several people in succession arguing with Dorothy Parker-Styles. Popular, she was not.'

'Did she argue with Grace? Only I heard the police took her in for questioning,' said Roz.

Honestly, Roz's network never failed to astound me. After all, I was the one who had a plant in the station, but her friendship with Sally Wright on the reception desk meant she learned all about the comings and goings of suspects and victims.

'Not exactly,' I said. 'But Dot and some others made remarks about foreigners.'

'Was the fair organised by the Nationalist Party to raise funds?' said Roz.

'No, but a lot of the dealers are set in their ways. Grace said she was used to it, but I'm not convinced. She's highly educated and comes from high society in Hong Kong. I doubt she ever experienced discrimination over there. At least until China took over. The look in her eyes when Dot insulted her would have scared anyone.'

'How awful,' said Ghita, who threatened to turn tearful.

I wondered if she knew all too well how Grace felt. She sniffed, and I handed her a tissue.

'And the murder?' said Roz.

'I went in on Sunday morning early to help Grace redo the table. She had found Dot's body in the storage area. It had been stabbed—'

My cell phone rang, and I tipped up my handbag to find it quicker. Roz tutted and rolled her eyes. I frowned at her.

'It could be important,' I said.

'It's probably Mouse telling you he overslept again,' said Roz.

I checked the screen.

'It's Flo. Hi Flo. I'm at the Vintage with Roz and Ghita. Are you nearby?'

'No, I'm at the station. I thought you might like to know the origin of the weapon we found sticking out of our victim.'

No-one except Mouse knew about the photograph I had taken, so I played along. Even Flo might take a dim view of me taking my own crime scene photographs.

'What have you found out?'

I listened while she told me everything I already knew, nodding even though she couldn't see me.

'That's fascinating. I suppose one of the stall holders lost their temper and used their stock.'

'Maybe. It's a precise stab though, direct to the heart. It looks more like a calculated blow than a hot-tempered lunge. I'll be doing the full autopsy in the next day or two. I've just got to finish up one I'm doing for D.I. Antrim in Brighton.'

'Give him my regards. On second thoughts, don't. He might not appreciate it.'

'I'll let you know if I find anything relevant. George knows I'm as leaky as a sieve. He won't mind as long as it's you. He told me you were helping.'

'It's easier to help him if I know the basics. Thanks Flo. Come and have coffee soon. We miss you.'

When I looked up, Roz and Ghita were staring intently at me.

'What kind of knife did they use to stab Dot with?' said Roz.

'I'm not investigating the murder this time. I'm leaving that to George.'

'What about Grace?' said Ghita.

'She didn't do it,' I said.

'Are you sure? What did Flo say?' said Roz.

'Flo told me the dagger was an athame.'

'And what on earth is that?' said Ghita.

'I'm not sure. But it has associations with witchcraft. I've never heard that term before. Have you?'

Roz stood up. She had gone pale.

'Um, I forgot something at home. Ed's, um, anyway, I've got to go. See you soon.'

Before either of us could react, she had bounded down the stairs and out of the shop.

'What was that about?' I said.

'Maybe she felt Ed's presence on shore,' said Ghita, giggling.

'Maybe she did.'

I got home to find Harry waiting for me. Mouse had a grin as wide as Christmas and even Hades had roused himself from his Lloyd Loom laundry basket to purr and yowl in pleasure. My heart almost burst with happiness. I missed Harry like a limb or an organ. Since he had reconciled with his brother, we had seen less of each other while they rebuilt their relationship. I understood how important it was to him, but his absence took much of the joy from my life. He held out his muscular arms and enveloped me in a tight hug. I kissed his bald pate, revelling in the feel of his stocky body next to mine where it belonged.

'Did you miss me?' he said.

'Not really.'

'She's lying. She pined like a princess,' said Mouse.

'Would the princess like to clear out Prince Charming's castle?' said Harry.

'We've got a castle clearance?' I said.

'Not exactly. He's aristocracy, but baronet rather than duke. Can you manage it tomorrow?'

'She's too busy finding bodies,' said Mouse. 'Again.'

Harry let go of me and held me at arm's length.

'Not again. Am I contaminating the crime scene?'

'Grace found the body, not me. I just found her finding it.'

Harry laughed.

'Oh, well, that's all right then. What on earth happened this time?'

'Somebody stabbed the unpleasant manager of the Vintage and Antique fair and left the body in the dealers' storage area behind the town hall.'

'Is George on the case?'

'Yes…'

'I hear a large "but" coming.'

Mouse sniggered.

'Does her butt look big in this?'

'You're not funny,' I said.

'He is quite,' said Harry. 'What's for supper? I'm starving.'

'There's spag bol in the fridge.'

'Perfect. I'll pick up a bottle of red wine, and you can tell me all about it when I get home.'

Chapter 9

Harry and I set out the next morning through driving rain, which made us slow to a crawl. The windscreen wipers struggled against the constant cascade of water streaming down the glass. The constant thunder made Harry jumpy, a reminder perhaps of his army service. He did not comment, but his hands were white on the steering wheel. Our almost identical taste in music made it easy for me to know how to change the mood. I put 'Riders on the Storm' by The Doors on the CD player, which eased the tension in his body. He relaxed and smiled at me in thanks.

He drove due north out of Seacastle in light traffic, past the Sainsbury's superstore where I did our weekly shopping. It triggered me into making a list in my notebook of the things I needed to buy on our way home. Harry rolled his eyes.

'I thought you were leaving the murder investigation to George?'

'I am.'

'Why are you making notes in your Poirot notebook then?'

'It's a shopping list.'

'Seriously? Aren't you a tiny bit curious about the murder? It seems right up your street, happening at a vintage fair and all. And with Grace involved, well…'

I knew he was right, but I still felt irritated by the question.

'George told me to leave it to him. I feel like I owe him that much, and Helen will be cross if I interfere.'

'What about Grace? She's not off the hook yet. I thought you were friends.'

'We are. That's why I'm steering clear. She's a private person, and she doesn't want me investigating her. I'm sure they'll find she has nothing to do with it.'

Harry raised an eyebrow, but he swallowed whatever he planned on saying.

'Fair enough. Keep an eye out for signs to Findon Hall, will you?'

I put away my notebook, but not before I wrote an updated list of the suspects and left a blank column for motives. Dorothy did not have too many allies at the fair. I wondered who hated her enough to finish her off in such a brutal way. I couldn't stop my mind working on the problem, even when I had promised not to.

Findon Hall sat glowering under the shadow of several magnificent Cedars of Lebanon, whose wide foliage cast shade over the gardens and dimmed the light at the windows. I wondered if the person who had planted them had been aware of the size and spread of the mature trees. I had once collected pine cones from cedars at Highgate Cemetery, which leaked resin on my favourite coat and stained it permanently. They found their way into the dustbin shortly afterwards. The building had Georgian facades, but, like many British stately homes, appeared to be a mishmash of styles and fashions added to by succeeding generations. I could imagine the rabbit warren of passageways created by the constant addition of annexes and improvements.

Sir Dudley Seagrove waddled out to greet us, surrounded by an entire pack of barking dogs of different breeds and sizes. He shouted at them to shut up, his red cheeks wobbling with effort, but they continued to bark and wag their tails in excitement even when he threatened to hit them.

'Sorry,' he said. 'They were my mother's. I don't think she ever disciplined them. They are great guard dogs, though.'

'No need to apologise,' said Harry. 'We like dogs.'

I fought my way through the pack to shake his hand and he gave me a wistful glance, which told me the pack had also kept any prospective girlfriends away.

'The stuff is in the annex at the back,' he said. 'I'm converting it into a separate flat, so I need to empty the area out before the builders arrive.'

'Do you have a price in mind?' said Harry.

'I'll pay you to take it away if you want,' said Sir Dudley. 'It's all got to go.'

I exchanged glances with Harry and crossed my fingers, hopeful of a good haul. We hadn't had much luck lately. Either someone else beat us to the best clearances, or we found unsuitable or scrapheap furniture we didn't want. Clearing houses was a real lottery. If you didn't turn up, you had no chance, but if you did, the chances of a win were tiny. I did not feel encouraged by the parlous state of the house. The rich trappings could not disguise the dilapidated interior. Paint peeled from walls and windows rattled with the least wind.

I followed Sir Dudley, keeping Harry between me and him, to his obvious disappointment. His cheeks were purple with exertion by the time we entered the annex, despite it being a short distance.

'Well, there you are. I'll leave you to it, shall I? Or would you like me to help you?' he said, wheezing.

I doubted Sir Dudley had ever lifted anything larger than a double gin and tonic, but I smiled.

'That's sweet of you, but we can manage. If you could rustle up a pot of tea, that would be lovely.'

His face lit up.

'I'll get Mrs Potts to whip up a pot right away. Toodle pip.'

'Did he really say toodle pip?' said Harry.

'I'm afraid so. Well, he's gone for now. Let's search.'

The annex comprised four rooms, two up and two down and I could imagine it making a lovely place to live. A conservatory had been tacked onto its outside wall which faced out onto the part of the gardens not thrown into shadow by the cedars, As I stepped into it, I took in the set of Lloyd Loom chairs and sofa and matching tables still in their original faded gold colour with their seat covers unrestored. There were even original matching cushions sitting squashed on the chairs where the last occupant had left their mark. I wondered if Lady Seagrove had left her last ghostly presence in the cushions, which would only evaporate if they were plumped back into shape.

'My mother loved to sit out here,' said Dudley, who had crept up behind me with the quiet stealth of a big cat.

He ran his hand along the back of the sofa and sighed.

'I guessed. You must miss her. Are you sure you don't want this furniture? It's all the rage.'

'No thanks. I'm already surrounded by centuries of junk in the main house. I'd like a modern family to move in here and bring the place into the twenty-first century. It would be nice to have some children playing in the garden, even if they're not my own.'

His voice had risen in pitch and I didn't dare look around.

'It must be quite lonely living here,' I said. 'Do you have any friends in the area?'

'Not really. Since the hunt got closed down, a lot of our social life dried up. The Hunt Balls used to be wonderful. My mother loved to entertain. But now, well, you know, it's not PC anymore, and most of my friends went to London in Mrs T's time and never came back.'

I hadn't expected to feel sorry for someone so privileged, but his loneliness was palpable.

'What was your mother like?'

'Wonderful. My father died of cancer when I was quite young, but she kept the house going. Unfortunately, she became rather batty in her old age. She had lost her marbles in the end. She claimed to be a witch. I found her sneaking out to the Cissbury Ring several times.'

'The Cissbury Ring? Isn't that a Celtic ring fort?'

'Yes, it's nearby. It's rather splendid, you know. It dates back over five thousand years. I'm told it's the largest hill fort in Sussex.'

'Didn't they used to mine flint up there?' said Harry, who had joined us.

Sir Dudley beamed with pleasure.

'They did. As a matter of fact, I have a rather nice collection of Neolithic axe heads and spear tips, if you are interested? Why don't you come and have a cup of tea and I'll take them out to show you? I'm planning on donating them to the Seacastle museum.'

'Fantastic,' said Harry.

'Are you an army man?' said Sir Dudley. 'Only they excavated a large anti-tank ditch around the fort in 1940 and positioned anti-aircraft guns across the highest part of the ridge too.'

'I never knew that.'

I watched them depart for tea, leaving me in their wake as they discussed the merits of the fortifications. Personally, I suspected the Nazis would have laughed at us for our pathetic attempt at defence, but what did I know? It pleased me to think Dudley could share his passions with someone interested, even if just for an hour. Harry loved to talk about the army too. I think he found it therapeutic to talk to other men about it. I looked around the now deserted conservatory with its ghostly cushions. I would also do well from the hoard of Lloyd Loom furniture and I had spotted a small chest of drawers that I knew I could flog to Grace and Max. A rather successful trip.

Chapter 10

I made Harry stop at Sainsbury's on the way home and did a quick shop for the Grotty Hovel. I also bought milk and coffee beans for Second Home. Mouse came outside to the street to help unload the van into the shop. He and Harry moved the furniture inside as fast as they could while I made room for it and kept one eye out for the traffic warden. Unloading stock at a business premises allowed us fifteen minutes of leeway for stopping on a single yellow line in Seacastle, although I hadn't seen this regulation written down. The fines for illegal parking were ferocious and immutable. I lived in dread of being pinged by our local warden who delighted in fining everyone for the slightest infraction. I presumed she worked on commission. No one enjoys their work that much.

Once Harry had parked the van and paid the meter, he returned to help Mouse and me carry the tables and chairs up to the café. The Lloyd Loom furniture looked fabulous in the Vintage just as I had expected. I felt tempted to use it permanently, but part of the fun of the Vintage rested on the clientele being able to buy their chair or table or a set if they wanted to. Several clients had done that after drinking their coffee, so I priced up the new pieces while Harry made us coffee. I noticed he seemed sombre after our trip, frowning and drawing his eyebrows together as he sipped his drink.

'I felt sorry for Sir Dudley,' he said. 'Poor bloke seems rather lonely in that big house of his.'

'Me too. I don't imagine he expected to miss his mother that much. It hits everybody hard,' I said.

'I might go up to Cissbury with him one day for a trip around the fortifications. Do you want to come with us?'

'I do,' said Mouse. 'If I'm invited.'

'Definitely,' I said. 'The views from the top of the fort are fabulous.'

The shop's bell clanged loudly as somebody forced the door open. It had been sticking because of the wood swelling in the damp air. I hadn't wanted to shave it down as it would have been too loose when it dried out again. I peered down the stairs and to my surprise Veronica Higgins stood beside the cash desk wringing her hands. I went down to greet her, and she turned eyes swollen with crying to me.

'I need your help,' she said.

'My help? I don't understand.'

'My friend Delia Dawson told me you're a private detective.'

'Not really. I mean, I dabble, but not officially.'

Veronica glared at me.

'I expect you learned it from your husband. He's only gone and arrested my Sid. I'm at my wit's end.'

'Why don't you come upstairs and have a coffee with me? You can tell us all about it.'

Veronica looked around in alarm.

'Are there other people here?'

'Yes, but they work on my cases too. You don't have to worry about them.'

She followed me up the stairs, looking behind her as if she thought somebody had followed her. If she hung around with Delia Dawson, she knew some dodgy folk. I wondered what Sid had been up to that made George have him arrested. From what I had observed at the fair,

Sid had the shifty look of someone who expected a hand on his collar at any moment, a look his wife had also perfected. After serving her tea with two sugars and a piece of cake—'Don't mind if I do,' she said—I asked her why the police had arrested her husband.

'It's the daggers,' she said. 'Sid only took them as a favour to his brother-in-law. They're cheap knock-offs. Chinese, I think. We put them on the stand, mixed in with the genuine articles. We weren't trying to cheat no one. There's not an expert out there who'd be fooled by them.'

'Were they athames?' said Mouse.

'Is that some sort of ninja sword? I don't think so.'

Harry gave me a sidelong glance and sucked his cheek in.

'What were they made of?' I asked.

'Some sort of plastic, I think. You couldn't stab anyone with them. The blade would snap off.'

She sniffed.

'Victimisation, that's what it is. Sid ain't done nothing wrong.'

Apart from selling cheap knock-offs as the real thing, I thought, though that's hardly a terrible crime. I remembered the fake Chanel bag I had bought on Brick Lane when I worked as an investigative reporter. I had sworn to buy myself the genuine article when I made a fortune, but somehow that date kept slipping into the future.

'Of course not,' I said, in my most soothing tone of voice. 'What can I do to help?'

'I need you to investigate about the murder, find out who done it, cos it weren't Sid.'

'Do you have any suspects?' I asked.

'Not exactly. Well maybe…'

'Tell me.'

'Well, I heard somebody used a dagger to kill Dot, and it might be one of ours. We had something similar to the knock-offs on our stand, a proper dagger with a black wooden handle. I remember seeing something like snakes on the hilt. Only it disappeared before the sale, you see.'

'Are you sure?'

'Oh yes. Jasper Christie gave it to me to sell. He said it were the genuine article. I could've sold it for a pretty penny, but somebody pinched it while we were off having a coffee at the café.'

'You didn't see them?'

'No, but I'm pretty sure I know who took it. He had been admiring it earlier before Dot threw him out.'

'Roy Loveday?'

'I'm not a nark. I wouldn't tell the police anything, but my Sid, he's delicate, you know. He won't be happy in the cells.'

I hid a smile.

'I'm sure he's not. But why would Roy Loveday want to kill Dot?'

'She took his table away, didn't she? Roy was furious. You saw him.'

'Murdering her seems over the top, don't you think? There are lots of other fairs just as good as this one.'

'He hated that family. They had history.'

'What sort of history?'

'I'm not sure. Miles Quirk would know. He and Dot went way back.'

She took a large slurp of tea and wiped the back of her mouth on her sleeve.

'Will you take the case? I can pay you in kind. You can put them in the display cabinet,' she said.

Visions of a row of dangerous knives lying on the cushions of the display cabinet appeared before my eyes. I coughed and avoided Mouse's startled expression.

'Um, that's okay. My friend Grace already asked me to help her find out what happened. She's also a suspect you know.'

Veronica nodded.

'Well, that's hardly surprising, is it? Her being Chinese and all. They can be so inscrutable.'

I felt as if I should disinfect the chair she had used and count the silver spoons after she left. Her casual racism made my blood boil. But her comments about Roy Loveday and Miles Quirk had made me think. I couldn't recall Miles returning from his meeting after the incident with the plate. He seemed fond of Abigail. Maybe she knew where to find him.

Chapter 11

Harry and I attended Dot's funeral and see if we could pick up any clues to her brutal demise. The service took place at the charming Norman parish church near her home, just outside Findon, north of Seacastle.

'I recognise this road,' I said.

'They were neighbours. Maybe Dot knew Lady Seagrove.'

'She must have done. I wonder if Dud knows anything about her past.'

'We need to make a date to explore the fort with him. It will be the perfect time to ask him a few questions in relaxed surroundings.'

The small church featured oak benches flanking a tiled nave. Stained glass windows with depictions of saints and knights filtered the weak sunlight, which struggled to light the interior. A smell of candle wax and mothballs permeated the air of the church. Dot's coffin rested on trestles in the chancel between the seating intended for the choir. From the size of the seats, I imagined it had been built for small boys. I recognised Sir Dudley's broad back in one of the front pews inside the church, which was bursting at the seams with local gentry. I saw none of them in Seacastle, but I recognised some faces from antique fairs I had attended in the past before I concentrated on vintage goods.

Harry and I sat in the back row and watched a procession of worthies damning Dot with faint praise from the pulpit. I noticed no one seemed sad, nor could they dredge up too many nice things to say about her. Harry turned to whisper in my ear, causing several people to turn around and stare at us.

'Seems like she was as popular as a dose of the—'

'Shut up. You shouldn't speak ill of the dead.'

'Sorry. Force of habit. Army banter.'

While I listened to the mourners drowning Dot in a litany of clichés, my brain worked overtime. Why had the murderer chosen to kill Dot at that time, and in such a public place? Was it a warning to someone else, or a public display of revenge? Dot appeared to be universally disliked, but that's not a good enough reason to kill someone. I wondered if she had seen it coming and begged for mercy. Probably not. I doubt she believed anyone had the guts to murder her. That would explain the look of pained surprise frozen on her features when Grace found her.

Just as the wooden bench felt unbearably hard, the service drew to a close. Harry and I waited until most of the mourners had filed past us before leaving our bench and following them out of the church. Sir Dudley spotted us and waddled over, his face pink with pleasure. He shook Harry's hand and kissed mine.

'I didn't realise you knew Dot,' he said. 'She was an old friend of my mother's. They used to sneak off together at night. They thought I didn't realise, but they weren't quiet about it.'

'Did you know Dot well?' I asked.

He shook his head.

'She had no interest in me,' he said. 'I wasn't one of the chosen few.'

'I'm surprised she got on with anyone,' said Harry.

At that moment, Abigail approached us, her black mourning suit hanging off her bony frame. She smiled shyly at Dudley who swallowed and struggled to get any words out.

'Ah, Abigail, do you know these two?' he asked.

'Yes, no, at least I've met Tanya.'

'I'm Harry Fletcher, at your service.'

She giggled and proffered her hand.

'Abigail Parker-Styles, at yours.'

She ignored me for the next five minutes, batting her eyelids at Harry and Dudley, and braying with nervous laughter. I found her behaviour a little disturbing, fake even, but I couldn't be sure. We were after all at her aunt's funeral. Perhaps she hid a myriad of emotions under the false gaiety. Her reaction to Dot's body had been peculiar to say the least. I wondered who she imagined had murdered her aunt. She had crowed about the murder and assumed it had been a revenge killing for the death of her mother. I needed to investigate Felicity's accident.

Then a man in the crowd caught my eye. He had a large-brimmed hat on which he had angled down to hide his face. His scarf had been tied high on his neck so that only a small portion of his face was visible. The wind lifted the brim for an instant and I realised who it was. Roy Loveday! Why on earth had he come to Dot's funeral? It made no sense. I watched him as he hovered on the edge of the crowd, as if trying to decide whether or not to approach someone. He looked across and saw me staring at him. In an instant, he had turned and disappeared again. I felt like I had imagined it.

The mourners moved away from the church down a narrow pathway to the graveyard where the coffin had been placed on sturdy wooden planks over a newly dug grave. A single raven alighted on the coffin and Abigail gasped behind us.

'A harbinger of doom,' she said.

'Actually, it signifies an impending shift in consciousness, inviting you to explore your inner realms,' said Dudley.

He noticed us staring at him.

'That's what my mother claimed anyway,' he said, and then excused himself to find a better spot close to the head of the coffin.

Harry raised an eyebrow at me, and I shrugged. Lots of people behave strangely at a funeral, and Dot's interment had brought a lot of unspoken feelings to the surface, given how abrasive she had been in life. Dudley appeared to be affected by it all, more than Abigail, but then she seemed to have lost interest in the burial and flirted with Harry instead. Dot had outraged and alienated many people. I wondered why they had bothered to turn up at her funeral. Perhaps they wanted to make sure she had gone.

After Dot had been lowered into the grave, we joined the mourners heading to Findon Manor. I hadn't been expecting such a magnificent building, equal in splendour to the Seagrove place, and about the same era. The drawing room had been cleared to make a central space in which to congregate, and trays of canapes lay on tables and sideboards surrounding it. A jaded looking butler served cups of tea from a battered urn, disappointing those who had expected something stronger. I took one and swigged it down, asking for a refill almost immediately. He gave me a thin-lipped smile.

The noise level rose as the mourners filled the room. I noticed Abigail had sunk to the sofa, looking sad and lost. I crossed the floor and sat beside her, taking her hand.

'Are you okay?' I said. 'This is all rather a shock for you, isn't it?'

She nodded.

'I don't know how you will feel about this, but I'm investigating your aunt's death. Is it okay if I ask you a couple of questions?'

'Aren't the police doing that?'

'Well, yes, but one of the stall holders asked me if I would help her. The police have arrested her husband.'

'Sid Higgins? Oh, he didn't do it,' she said. 'He's a petty thief, not a murderer. He doesn't have the gumption.'

'The day your aunt was murdered, you said the devil had come for her. What did you mean?'

'I thought it was obvious. She murdered my mother. It was time she paid the piper.'

'Didn't your mother die in a car crash?'

'Supposedly.'

'Do you remember what happened?'

'Of course, I was in the car too.'

'But weren't you a baby at the time?'

She snorted.

'I was three, but I remember it like it was yesterday.'

'Can you tell me what you remember? If it's not too traumatic for you.'

'It's always traumatic for me, but I'll tell you over a drink. Let's head to the sitting room for a gin and tonic. Tea is for losers.'

I followed her through a side door into a cosy sitting room with ancient armchairs and a fireplace still full of ash and the stub ends of burnt logs. Abigail opened an Art Deco cocktail cabinet and sloshed a good helping of gin into two glasses. She added the bare minimum amount of tonic and handed me one glass.

'Bottoms up,' she said. 'Don't let the bugs bite.'

'They'd get drunk if they bit me after this,' I said, and she laughed.

'Lightweight. Where were we? Oh yes, my dead mother. Well, I remember it being dark. My mother had put me on the back seat with a seat belt on. She drove too fast, and I was afraid. The seatbelt didn't fit me and I pulled it under my arm to stop it from hitting my face. While I fiddled with the belt, I felt the car lurch off the road and hit something hard. We turned upside down, and I was hanging from the belt. I could see my mother's head bleeding. I shouted for help until my throat wouldn't work. Then somebody came. They took me out of the car. I don't know who. They had a black cape on. It covered their face. They put me on the grass. Then I saw the car on fire. My mother did not come out. I couldn't move because my leg was broken. I watched the car burn until they came to rescue me.'

'You must have been very frightened.'

'I think I was too shocked to take it in.'

'And you don't know who took you out of the car?'

'No, but I think it must have been Dot. She had one of those capes. She hated my mother for getting pregnant. I think she set fire to the car.'

'But you don't know?'

'I'm as sure as I can be. I saw the tattoo on her arm, but I only remembered years later when I did therapy. I thought Dot had rescued me, but she had killed my mother too.'

'What did the tattoo depict?'

Abigail swallowed the rest of her gin and looked away from me.

'I don't remember.'

I ruminated on the story Abigail had told me all the way home, turning it over and over in my mind. Abigail had only been four at the time and she had been in a serious car crash. She could have been hallucinating. But what if they were repressed memories caused by the trauma of seeing her mother in the burning car? Her lie about the tattoo seemed to me to be pretty transparent. She avoided my eyes and threw back her drink to distract me, but she didn't fool me. She knew what tattoo Dot had on her arm. Could it be connected with her death?

Harry coughed, interrupting my chain of thought.

'Hello, Earth to Tanya. Are you receiving me?'

His voice brought me down with a bump.

'Of course. Did you ask Dudley to come to Cissbury Ring with us?'

'Yes. Um, Abigail insisted on coming too.'

'Oh. Can't be helped I suppose. In fact, it may be helpful. Dot and Dudley's mother got up to many escapades together, if you believe Dudley. Perhaps we can find out more about Dot and why someone killed her. I need to ask Flo about the autopsy too.'

'Won't George throw a fit?'

'Who's going to tell him? Anyway, I only have one question which will have a one-word answer. He can't object to that.'

'Hm. I'm not sure George will see it that way.'

Chapter 12

The next morning, I found Mouse bleary eyed at the kitchen table. He had made himself some toast, which he nibbled with caution. Hades tried to sit on his lap, but Mouse brushed him off. Hades did not take kindly to this and marched to the cat flap and out into the garden, scattering the sparrows who were conferring under the brambles.

'Hung over?' I asked.

'I may die.'

'You look ghastly. Where were you last night?'

'Goose's wife let him out for the evening, so we headed to the Shanty and met the rest of the lads.'

'And the rest is history?'

'I'm afraid so. Please, will you make me a bacon sandwich?'

'Nature's remedy for a hangover? Okay. Sit tight.'

I made one for each of us. Harry, who had woken up grumpy, refused to come down for breakfast. He insisted on eating his sandwich in bed. I agreed on the condition he shook out all the crumbs when he got up. Both of my menfolk being out of sorts; I got on with my day and left them to it. First, I phoned Flo.

'Hi Tanya. I can guess why you're calling me, but I can't tell you anything about the autopsy or George will murder me too.'

'Just one question, I promise. You only have to give me a one-word answer.'

'One word?'

'Well, maybe two, but one of them could be a.'

I heard her sigh.

'Ask me.'

'Did Dot have a tattoo?'

'Yes.'

'What of?'

'That's two questions.'

'No, it isn't. Not really. I should have asked you what Dot's tattoo was first. I knew she had one already.'

Another sigh.

'A pentagram.'

'A pentagram?'

'That's what I said. Can I go now?'

'Yes. Thank you. I—'

She had rung off. I would have to have her for supper soon and fill her with wine. Flo could be a little sensitive if she thought I was taking advantage of her. The knowledge that Dot had a tattoo of a pentagram on her arm perturbed me, as I had no idea why she would have done this. Dot had struck me as rigidly conservative in her manner, speech and dress, not the sort of person who would consider having a tattoo at all. I tended to associate them with people who didn't conform to old-fashioned norms. They had spread rapidly among younger people in the last few years, but Dot did not qualify as someone who might have followed a fad. And why have a pentagram?

I was still puzzling about this as I polished the tables in the Vintage. I had left the men at home with strict instructions to do internet searches on Roy Loveday, Jasper Christie and Miles Quirk and to find out where they were lurking. The work distracted me for a short time before I picked up my phone and looked up pentagrams. I soon found a reference and sat upstairs with a coffee, reading how it served as a symbol of Wiccan Faith and represented earth, air, water, fire and spirit. Its major use seemed to be as a charm to protect against evil forces, especially if it was surrounded by a circle. I felt bemused when I realised its prominent use in witchcraft. What had any of this got to do with pompous Dorothy Parker-Styles? It didn't make any sense. Maybe she had a wild era during her teenage years?

The shop bell clanged and rattled downstairs and I heard Roz call up to me. She ran up the stairs full of beans and made herself a coffee.

'You'll never guess what,' she said, wiping the foam off her lip. 'I heard the weirdest thing about...'

She trailed off and frowned.

'What's up? You've got a strange expression on your face. Have you had a fight with Harry?'

'No, nothing like that. I'm perplexed. Flummoxed.'

'Can I help?'

'I'm not sure. Do you know anything about pentagrams or witchcraft?'

Her face paled.

'Why are you asking me?'

'Because you're here and I need help. Do you remember I said Dot was murdered using an athame?'

'Yes. So what?'

'Well, that's a witch's dagger, and Dot had a pentagram tattoo on her arm. It can't be a coincidence.'

Roz stood up and walked to the front window of the Vintage. She pretended to have seen something in the street, but she was playing for time. She had no talent for hiding her feelings. I could tell she was wrestling with herself, so I didn't speak. A seagull flashed by the window yelling abuse about something and I caught the flash of yellow on its beak. Roz turned around.

'It isn't. There's a coven of witches who live in and around Seacastle. They have a long history, but few people know about them. They keep their allegiances quiet.'

'How do you know about them then?'

Roz flushed. I couldn't believe it. I never recalled seeing her react like that before to a question. She had always been straightforward with me, too honest on occasion. She picked at her sleeve.

'I've dabbled.'

'Dabbled? What does that mean?'

'In my teens. I tried to join them.'

It shouldn't have surprised me. Roz did not belong on this planet. If she had announced her real identity as Vondra from Venus, I would not have batted an eyelid. I bit my lip.

'Like the army?' I said.

'Don't mock me. I had a calling.'

'Why wouldn't they let you join? I'd have thought you were the ideal candidate.'

'I know right? I studied the Wicca lore until I was blue in the face, but they would not accept me for initiation. I don't know why. They never explained why I didn't qualify.'

'They were wrong. You'd have been a splendid witch.'

'Well, I am a sea witch. But that's different.'

'I'm sure. Look, I can tell it's a personal matter for you, but I would like to find out what happened to Dot. She wasn't the nicest person on the planet, but nobody deserves to die like that. And Grace is still under suspicion. We need to discover the truth if we can. Is there anyone who can help us?'

'There's a witch in Brighton who belongs to the same coven. She owns a spiritual shop on a side street selling crystals and pentagrams and other paraphernalia. Her name's Perpetua Hastings. She might talk to us if I ask her.'

'That would be great. This case is stranger by the minute.'

'How did you know about Dot?'

'Abigail claims she saw the tattoo when Dot rescued her from a burning car. I'm not sure I believed her. She was only four at the time and she says Dot left her own sister, Felicity, to die in the car crash. Flo confirmed Dot has the tattoo, but I'm not at all sure Abigail told me the truth. She's an odd sort of person, prone to hysteria and exaggeration.'

'I'd be odd if I'd seen my mother die in a car crash.'

'We should investigate the cause of the crash too. I'll get my little hacking Mouse to have a look in the files. Could you give Perpetua a call and see if she'd meet with us? Meanwhile, I'll text Mouse to start digging.'

Chapter 13

Roz refused to come and meet Perpetua Hastings with me, which I understood, and I did not force the issue. I considered asking Harry, but his utter disbelief in the supernatural made me think he might just scoff at her crystals. Ghita refused to meet a witch, citing her fear of the supernatural. I could not persuade her of the essential good nature of witches, as she had seen too many scary movies. It occurred to me that Grace might like to be involved. The police had not interviewed her again, but George had told me she remained on their list of suspects. I found it hard to fathom how she hadn't been eliminated yet, but she took it calmly. It made her determined to help me with the case. She had an interest in different beliefs springing from the enforced atheism of her childhood. When I mentioned the possibility of meeting a witch, she jumped at the chance.

'A real witch. Is there such a thing?' she asked.

'Mouse did a little research for me. Apparently, witches are common all over the world, but they follow different traditions. The members of the original British covens were slaughtered hundreds of years ago during the witch trials, but Wicca magic became popular in the 50s and 60s spawning whole new generations of witches who set up their own covens.'

'But what's witchcraft for?'

'I really know nothing about it. We can ask.'

Perpetua Hastings' shop, Practical Magic, sat on a cross street in the centre of Brighton. A sign outside advertised a sale on potion phials and ingredients. Grace cooed with pleasure and took a selfie in front of the sign. The bow window at the front had faux bubbles in the glass, giving it an antique look, but making it impossible to see inside. We stepped through the door into a wonderland of eccentric items. The smell of essential oils almost knocked me out at first, but I soon got used to it and gazed around at the sea of candles, incense and spell books, grimoires and idols, herbal sachets and potion ingredients that were stacked on tables, shelves and in corners. One table had a covering of divination tools like crystal balls, tarot cards, and runestones (whatever they were).

Grace flitted between the tables, emitting small gasps of astonishment and adoration. I had never seen her so animated. We stared at the back wall. Hundreds of boxes of wands stacked to the ceiling like Ollivanders in Harry Potter. A flat glass display cabinet, similar to the one in Second Home, acted as a counter. We gazed into it at the row of athames, varying from the plain wooden ones to the elaborate ones with decorated hilts and hasps.

'I imagined nothing like this,' Grace exclaimed. 'It's amazing—some of these artefacts must be quite valuable antiques. Look at those statues.'

Just then, a woman in a flamboyant outfit—like Roz on acid—swept through the beaded curtain, striking a pose before turning to meet our gaze. She held a stuffed squirrel in one hand and a wand in the other. I couldn't tell if she had done it for effect, or if we had disturbed her while she was casting a spell of some sort. I wanted the squirrel for my Easter window display, but couldn't tell if it was for sale. I didn't want to offend her. She had already judged us as 'not fellow Wiccans'.

'I presume you are Tanya,' she said. 'And who is this?'

'I'm Grace Wong. It's an honour to meet you.'

Grace put her hands together and gave a slight bow. Perpetua's entire attitude changed from frosty to welcoming in a trice. I realised she had a standing we didn't appreciate and treated her like royalty.

'Thank you for seeing us at short notice,' I said. 'It's a privilege.'

She deigned to smile at us mere mortals.

'I'm glad you realise that,' she said, putting a closed sign on the door. 'Come through.'

We pushed through the beaded curtain into a chilly kitchen where Perpetua made a pot of herbal tea. I am not a fan of camomile, but I pretended to sip it with enthusiasm. Grace took one taste and left her cup on the table. Around us, packed onto shelves, were countless ancient books of magic and spells. I noticed a set of leather-bound volumes with dates on them running back at least two centuries. They appeared to be historical records belonging to the coven.

'You are friends of Roz. Poor girl. Somebody should have explained to her about us, but she dived in head first. We disappointed her.'

'She said nice things about you. That's why we're here.'

'It's about the murder, isn't it? A dreadful business, especially using an athame to stab her. Blasphemy. Now it's defiled, its power forever lost.'

'Can it be cleansed?' said Grace.

Perpetua's brow creased, and she rubbed her chin.

'That is a contentious question, with no simple answer. An athame used to kill is tainted or imbued with negative energy. The coven needs to agree to a special ceremony to reset and reconsecrate it.'

'I understand Dorothy Parker-Styles was a member of the same coven as you. How did she qualify as a member?'

'The Seacastle coven is a rare hereditary coven. It isn't common knowledge, but it is a branch of the New Forest Coven, which was the sole survivor of the witch trials. We follow the teachings of Gerald Gardner who was the founder of Gardnerian Wicca. Membership of the coven passes from mother to child.'

'What happens if more than one child is born?' said Grace.

'The coven will choose the successor.'

'The coven chose Dot over Felicity?' I said.

'Who ever told you that? Felicity was the chosen successor. She had all the qualities to make her a future leader of the coven. Dot only took over when Felicity died.'

'So Abigail is the rightful heir to Felicity's place in the coven?'

'She is, but…'

Perpetua picked up the stuffed squirrel and started rearranging the fur on its tail. We waited.

'Dot had shifted the ethos of the coven in ways that upset some members. She was money orientated instead of spiritual. Some valuable artefacts belonging to the coven are missing. Abigail has been tainted by Dot. I have never spoken to her.'

'Do you think she sold them?' said Grace. 'They could be worth a fortune if they come from the original coven in the 17th century.'

'We aren't interested in money. Their spiritual worth is incalculable. If Dot sold them, she didn't just betray our history; she damaged our future. For many of us, that is unforgivable—utter sacrilege.'

'How much does Abigail know about this?'

'Only as much as Dot told her. I suspect she is in the dark.'

'Does she know Dot usurped her position in the coven?'

'I couldn't tell you, but someone might know.'

'Is it possible to give me their name?'

'I don't see why not. Membership is not a secret, but I beg you to be discreet. I think you met him already. He is Abigail's godfather.'

'Who's that?' I asked.

'Miles Quirk.'

'Miles? I never would have guessed.'

'His deep knowledge of antique rituals and artefacts makes him a valued member of the coven. He's the one who noticed the missing artefacts. He suspected Dot had swapped them out for similar ones which were less valuable.'

'And the other members?'

'Why don't you ask him? I feel uncomfortable telling you so much about us.'

'How I can get hold of him?'

'I can give you his card.'

'Could I persuade you to lend me the squirrel as well? I'll return it with a rabbit for interest.'

She laughed and shook her head.

'Are you sure you're not a witch?' she said. 'That's a genuine witch's joke.'

On our way back to Seacastle, Grace held the squirrel on her lap and stroked him absentmindedly. I felt as if I had left Perpetua's shop with more questions than answers about the coven's members and their powerful motivation for revenge. Dot's betrayal of their trust could have been a motive for her murder, with Miles or others within the coven seeking to reclaim what was stolen from them.

'What are you thinking?' said Grace.

'I'm wondering how I get Miles to step out of the shadows.'

'I've still got the plate,' she said. 'The one Miles wants. I can ask him to come to the shop.'

'I'm not sure it's ethical to extract information by using the plate as a bribe.'

'Who said anything about a bribe? He pays or I keep it.'

Chapter 14

Miles Quirk turned up at the Asian Antique Emporium about five minutes early for his appointment to pick up the plate. He sported an extraordinary violet corduroy suit over a black polo neck, complemented by a flamboyant scarf adorned with purple tulips tied in an artful knot to one side. He entered the shop with the energy of a coiled spring, ready for flight at the slightest excuse. The exquisite items on display soon captivated him, and he flitted from one to another, like a moth in a honeysuckle bush, emitting little sighs of wonder and approval. It reminded me of Grace's reaction to Perpetua's shop. Having observed him for a while, Grace approached, putting her hand on his arm and he jumped in fright, casting his eyes around for the door. She guided him to her corner table and patted the cushion on the armchair.

'Would you like some tea?' she offered. 'Perhaps a nice cup of jasmine?'

He nodded and then did a double take when he spotted me lurking behind the counter.

'An ambush?' he said. 'I've heard from Abigail that you're investigating Dot's murder. Who's paying you?'

'I'm not sure it's any of your business, but Veronica Higgins asked me to help her after the police arrested her husband.'

His eyes widened.

'Do you know why?'

'Something to do with a box of dodgy daggers. She's worried they're going to charge Sid with murder using the daggers as a pretext.'

He rolled his eyes.

'Those two are as bent as a nine-bob-note. But Sid didn't hate Dot. He even mentioned selling random things on his stall for her sometimes. Have you found any clues yet? There must be a multitude of suspects. It's ironic they chose an athame to do it, though.'

I debated asking him where he was on the day of the murder, but I decided to get the background straight first.

'Perpetua Hastings told us you are Abigail's godfather. Were you always close to Felicity?'

'As close as two unrelated people can be. Felicity was my universe. Nobody loved her like I did.'

I blinked.

'But aren't you—'

'Gay? What's that got to do with it? And I'm not Abigail's father, if that's what you're wondering. Flic was my muse.'

'You must have been devastated when she died,' said Grace.

'I almost went with her. But I had to look out for Abigail. Dot hadn't got a maternal bone in her body.'

'Abigail believes Dot murdered her mother,' I said 'Could Felicity's death have been related to the coven?'

Miles gave me a sidelong glance.

'Why do you ask me?'

'Aren't you a member?'

The blood drained away from his face.

'She shouldn't have told you,' he said. 'She had no right.'

He stood, and I thought he might leave, but Grace slid the Bawo and Dotter plate halfway across the table towards him, and he sat down again.

'Bribery?'

'It's not free,' said Grace.

'What is?'

He took another sip of his tea and sat back in the armchair, feigning relaxation.

'How long have you got?' he said. 'I suppose Perpetua told you how Dot took Flic's place in the coven?'

'Yes, she also told us that some members of the coven weren't happy about it.'

'You knew Dot. Can you imagine being happy about it? She was rotten to the core. She had no interest in nature, or spiritual life, or Wicca philosophy. She only wanted status and money. Look at the way she handled the antique fair, squeezing every penny out of the stallholders. Flic's role as guardian of our most important historical pieces meant they were kept at Findon Hall unless they were needed for a ceremony. She suspected Dot of having taken some of them to a valuer before returning them to the collection. We had planned to remove them all to my house before Flic died. I think Dot uncovered our plan.'

'Are you saying she murdered Flic to steal the artifacts?'

'I'm not saying anything. I have no proof. I only know Flic crashed in the dead of night with Abigail loose in the back seat. She never drove the car without strapping Abigail in.'

'What do you think happened?' said Grace.

'I don't know, but Abigail was thrown clear out of the car, which saved her life.'

I shook my head.

'Abigail says somebody with a tattoo rescued her from the car and left her mother to die in the flames.'

82

'That's not what happened. She wants it to be true because she hates Dot, but Dot didn't kill Flic.'

He took a deep breath and sighed it out.

'Who investigated the car accident?' I asked.

'Someone at Brighton. I think his name was Antrim. He's a detective now.'

I couldn't smother a smirk.

'I've heard of him.'

'That's all I know. Can I have my plate? It's all I could think about since the fair.'

Not Dot then. A thought struck me.

'What happened to you after Dot broke the other plate? You said you had a meeting.'

'I did.'

'But you didn't come back to the fair again. Is that normal? I'd have thought it's the ideal place for you to search for artifacts for your collection.'

'I couldn't face it, anyway…'

He trailed off and fiddled with his teaspoon.

'Anyway what?' said Grace.

'I don't suppose it matters now,' he said. 'I had met the manager of the building. She had had enough of Dot stiffing her on the receipts, so she was on the lookout for someone new to run the fair.'

'And you volunteered?'

'She asked me.'

'And what did you say?' said Grace.

'I told her I'd think about it. She wanted an answer right away, so I drove home to ask my partner about it. It would have been an enormous time commitment once a year.'

'What did you decide to do?'

'She called me that evening to withdraw the offer without giving a reason. I'm sure Dot had interfered somehow. She wouldn't let anyone take over her lucrative operation.'

'You must have been furious.'

'Wouldn't you have been? Dot hated anyone to succeed except for herself.'

'Did you kill her?'

'Someone else got there first.'

'Who would you nominate if you had to guess?'

'Roy Loveday. He hated Dot with a passion. I heard what happened when Dot took his table away and gave it to you two. He's a prime suspect in my eyes. And it's not just the table.'

'What do you mean?' said Grace.

'I suspect he's Abigail's father.'

A light went on in my head. So that's why he turned up at Dot's funeral. He must have hoped to talk to Abigail and tell her about his relationship with her mother. Did Roy also suspect Dot of killing Felicity? Had he taken his revenge? Veronica Higgins suspected him of stealing a knife from her table. But why now?

'Does she know?' I said, hiding my reaction.

Miles sighed

'As far as I'm aware, Abigail doesn't even know she is heir to the vacancy in our coven. It's my fault. I've failed her. Flic would be so disappointed in me.'

'Perhaps you should tell her before she finds out on her own?'

Chapter 15

After Miles Quirk had left the Emporium, I helped Grace by washing up the cups. She made me promise to keep her updated on the case. After bidding her farewell, I made my way back along the High Street to the Second Home. I found it hard to believe that Abigail knew nothing about her mother and aunt both being involved in the Seacastle Coven. She had struck me as a young woman who might harbour a grudge. But how far would she take it? I needed the official police report on Felicity's accident to make sense of the differing versions offered by Miles and Abigail. D.I. Antrim and I had history, but I had helped him on a case with positive results, so maybe he would be prepared to let me see the file. I called his number with some trepidation, but I needn't have worried. He answered immediately, his voice sounding warm as he gave me a cheery greeting.

'Tanya? How nice to hear from you! I'm in your vicinity today chasing down a lead, so you were on my mind.'

'Would you like to drop in to Second Home for a coffee? Ghita delivered a white chocolate and raspberry cake to the Vintage yesterday.'

'Are you attempting to bribe an officer of Her Majesty's government?'

'That depends on whether you're willing to grant me a favour I need from you.'

'Why am I not surprised? I'm just down the road from you. I'll park up and be with you shortly.'

To my surprise, I found myself quite excited at the prospect of seeing Terry Antrim again. We did not have the best start, but our last interactions had made me appreciate his intellect and drive. I couldn't help comparing him with George, which seemed a little unfair. George was the policeman's policeman; solid, dependable and dogged, but you would never have accused him of being intellectual. If I committed a crime, I knew who would solve it quicker.

The doorbell clanged, and D.I. Antrim stalked inside, the legs of his trousers flapping against his skinny calves. His head preceded his body, like a praying mantis watching for the criminal to make the slightest move to betray their presence. His face lit up with pleasure when he saw me and he grabbed my shoulders with his thin fingers. I thought he might kiss my cheek, but he panicked at the last moment and held me at bay.

'Ms Bowe. You are looking splendid,' he said. 'No doubt you are dying to pick my brains about some nefarious villain or other. Shall we have that coffee?'

He followed me upstairs and somehow folded his long limbs into an armchair.

'Can I have a double espresso please? We were on a surveillance last night and I'm wilting.'

I wondered why a senior officer like him would do that, but I didn't ask. He had a reputation for being thorough, so it didn't surprise me.

'What shenanigans have you got yourself involved with this time?' he said.

'It's about a case you attended many years ago—an accidental death in a car crash.'

'Really? Who died?'

'A young woman called Felicity Nash.'

He sipped his coffee and his eyes glazed over as he searched his memory. I cut him a piece of cake and placed it on the table in front of him.

'I haven't told you anything yet,' he said, pulling the plate towards him.

'Are you going to?'

'Perhaps. What do you want to know?'

'I expect you've already heard about the recent murder of Dorothy Parker-Styles?'

'Yes. A shocking business. George has his hands full with that case, according to my sources.'

He tapped the side of his nose in a droll manner.

'Felicity Nash was her sister.'

'Her sister? I had forgotten. What a tragic family.'

'I don't think it's a tragedy. Did you know Felicity was a witch, and Dot too?'

He nodded.

'It's our business to know these things. There has been a coven in this area for hundreds of years. They're a harmless bunch. They like to cast a circle up at the Cissbury Ring from time to time. We've had no trouble with them. What's your point?'

'Dot's murder might be connected to Felicity's accident. It would make more sense if the car had been sabotaged.'

'Felicity's accident was my first case as a Senior Investigating Officer. I had not long joined the force, but it being a Sunday night, I had to stand in for more senior officers who weren't at work. I remember most details as if it were yesterday. Some cases just stick in your mind.'

'Are you still sure it was an accident?'

He leaned forward and rested his chin on his enlaced fingers. I could feel myself reddening under his intense gaze.

'Explain your question.'

'I'm working on the theory that somebody intended for Felicity to die in that crash. She left the house in a great hurry with Abigail in the back of the car, but she didn't strap her in, which I am told was unheard of.'

He held up a finger to stop me from talking.

'Felicity couldn't have strapped Abigail in. I don't remember any child seat being found at the scene of the accident.'

'No car seat? But who removed it?'

'I don't know. It seems odd they would have removed it to harm a child.'

'Could someone have been waiting for Abigail to grow up before killing Dot?'

'It's impossible to say right now. From what I hear, George is overwhelmed by a sea of suspects. Dot did not suffer fools. She wouldn't have won any popularity contests.'

He frowned and scratched his head.

'There's something else I've remembered about the crash. Abigail was thrown from the car during the impact, which saved her life. However, paramedics found her laid out on the grass in what seemed to be a recovery position. They thought it was a coincidence.'

'Abigail says someone with a tattoo on their arm took her from the car before it caught fire. She claims they left her mother to die.'

'When did she tell you this? It's not on file or I'd remember it.'

'I don't know. We met at Dot's funeral and Abigail behaved strangely. She told me about her memory during the funeral tea, but she didn't say when she had remembered it. I assumed Dot's death had affected her worse than she expected, but maybe it's genuine recall.'

'Why would anyone be trying to kill Felicity?'

'Some members of the coven discovered Dot had been making inquiries about selling some of the coven's most precious artefacts to specialist dealers. I had wondered if Felicity had found out about Dot's attempts to sell their heritage and confronted her about it.'

'Are you suggesting Dot might have sabotaged the car to eliminate her and take over the coven?' he asked.

'She would have gained direct access to the heirlooms if she had been intent on selling them.'

'I don't recall any mechanical defects being mentioned, but I can bring up the original report and have a look for you if you like. We may need to re-open the case. I'll speak to George about doing a joint investigation.'

'Please don't let on where you got this info. George would have kittens.'

'Fair enough. But you'll need to give me your sources.'

'Will you keep me posted? I promise to update you on anything I find out.'

'It seems you are one step ahead of us, as usual. As long as you keep well clear of the prime suspects, I don't see what harm it can do.'

'Can you tell me who they are?'

'The slice of cake wasn't that big.'

Chapter 16

With D.I. Antrim promising to get back to me if he found any pertinent additional evidence about the cause of Felicity's car crash, I had time to review my notes on the case. Miles' revelations about Dot's intention to sell priceless artifacts belonging to the coven had added a further level of complexity to the investigation into her death. Perpetua had told me something similar, so I felt sure Dot's murder, at least, would be associated with the coven's heritage. I couldn't figure out if Felicity's accident had anything to do with this, but talking to Roy Loveday would be non-negotiable if we were to understand it. However, having seen Roy angry once, I did not intend to speak to him alone. I needed a pretext to set up a meeting. Veronica Higgins couldn't wait to provide me with one.

'He collects racing memorabilia. I'll ring him and tell him you've got something which he might like. Can you suggest something for him?'

'I'll see what I can do.'

I called Harry, knowing his uncle had left behind a cardboard box full of racing programmes from the 1800s, a set of famous jockey cigarette cards and some limited edition prints of races at various tracks. He also had a book on racing and steeple-chasing published by The Badminton Library in 1887. Harry had zero interest in these items and didn't mind selling them, but I made him ring his brother Nick first to see if he cared.

'More junk? No thanks,' he said.

So, we set out to meet Roy Loveday with the complete box, hoping his love of racing would allay his suspicions about our motives. Did Roy know I had spotted him at Dot's funeral? I would have to be cautious with my questions. Maybe he intended to find out what we knew. George had warned me against revealing evidence to suspects.

'It's like the dance of the seven veils,' he told me. 'Smoke and mirrors.'

George loved a mixed metaphor. He could murder a cliché too. I wondered how Helen fared with the constant stream of well-worn jokes and stories. At least she could empathise with me. My sister had not been the most sympathetic listener during the years I spent with George. Getting my own back felt good, albeit strange. The boot was on the other foot since they had got together. Even thinking about George made me spout clichés!

With Led Zeppelin thundering out of the dashboard, we rolled along to Roy's house outside Lewes, a post-war prefab that had seen better days. The tar paper roof had been patched more often than the road to Lancing. Tiny windows with stained curtains let in the bare minimum amount of light. It looked as if it had developed a lean and I hoped it would not decide to collapse while we were inside. Roy Loveday opened the front door a crack to peer out at us before pulling it open.

'Can't be too careful,' he said, scratching his arse.

I hoped he wouldn't offer to shake my hand later. I didn't want to offend him by refusing. As usual, Harry seemed immune to other people's foibles and gave him a cheery greeting. We cross the cracked linoleum floor, which creaked ominously, and sat on an uncomfortable couch with a plastic cover. I notice damp patches on the plywood walls and the rust on the window frames. Roy had not been making a fortune from selling antiques. Instead, he rotted along with his house.

Roy soon warmed to Harry's cockney humour and no-nonsense manner. He brewed up a strong pot of tea, which he served in chipped mugs. I hoped the boiling water had killed most of the germs already. While I sipped my tea, Harry took out the ephemera for Roy to peruse. He received each item with great reverence and examined it without hurry, his eyes shining with interest. The book about steeple chasing maintained his interest for several minutes as he scanned the tables and pictures. Having examined all the items, he went through them again, shuffling the sets of racing cards and replacing them in the box with exaggerated care.

'How much for the lot?' he said.

He muttered under his breath when Harry gave him a price, but he did not debate it, which I found interesting. When the box stood empty, Roy cleared his throat.

'I'm interested in buying the entire box, if you give me a fair price, but I'm pretty sure you came looking for information too. Maybe we can negotiate?'

'I'd like to ask you some questions about your relationship with the Parker-Styles sisters, if you don't mind,' I said.

'I don't. The police will invite me to the station soon, but that ex-husband of yours is slow off the blocks. Did he send you?'

'George? Heavens no. I'm a private investigator. Well, not officially, but anyway…'

I trailed off. I could hear how feeble I sounded. He took a big slurp of his tea, slopping some of it down his already food-stained t-shirt, and smirked at me.

'Ask away,' he said.

'I've been told you used to hang around with Felicity Nash? How did you first meet her?'

'Oh, I didn't meet her first. I started with Dot.'

He laughed at my jaw drop.

'Dot and I met at the track. We both loved horse racing and gambling and skipping school. We had some wild times together, but then I fell for Felicity at a party. Their mother had married twice, so the sisters had different surnames. I didn't know she was Dot's sister until it was too late. I didn't mean to, but I broke Dot's heart, and she blamed her sister.' He rubbed his chin, gazing out of the window as if looking into the past. 'Their relationship broke down after their mother died and the coven picked Flic as the heir. Dot had a criminal record by then.'

'A police record? What had she done?'

He shrugged.

'Nothing too serious. She sold fake antiques to a dealer, and he took her to court. She got three months in the nick. While she did time, I moved in with Flic.'

'Is that when you got her pregnant?'

He shifted in his seat and grimaced.

'You've been busy,' he said. 'Who told you that?'

'I'm not at liberty to say.'

'What happened next?' said Harry.

'I lost her. Flic threw me out because I wouldn't marry her. I was too young and too stupid, and she died because of me.'

His voice had thickened, and he struggled to get the words out.

'Why do you say that?' said Harry.

'I realised I had made a terrible mistake, but Flic wouldn't even let me see the baby. Dot blocked me from seeing either of them. I kept begging for forgiveness, but nothing worked.'

He wandered around the room as if chased by the memories.

'What did you do?' asked Harry.

'I worked as a mechanic in Southampton. I wrote to Flic the whole time, but I never got a reply.'

'That's harsh. Did you try again?'

'After I came home to Lewes, Flic contacted me, hysterical, one day. She had found a pile of my letters in the attic unopened. She told me Dot used Abigail to keep her trapped at home. I promised to rescue her.'

'Did she crash trying to escape?'

'I don't know. I guess so. It nearly killed me too. I've tried hard to forget her, but she was the love of my life. I've never found anyone else.'

'But then your mother worked with Dot in the antique fairs.'

'I found it hard to take, but it wasn't my mother's fault. She didn't know about Felicity and Abigail, and I never told her about Dot either.'

'You must have been furious when Dot cancelled your table for the fair.'

'I wanted to murder her. All my past resentment resurfaced.'

I didn't ask him the obvious question. He wouldn't have told me if he had killed her anyway.

'Did you go to Dot's funeral?' I asked.

'You saw me there? I thought so.'

'Why did you come?'

'I had hoped to speak to Abigail, but she unravelled after the service, and I thought it better to give her time to recover.' He shut his eyes lost in the moment. When he opened them again, he said, 'She looks like me, don't you think? Poor thing.'

'She does. There's no mistaking her father,' I said.

He beamed.

'You spoke to her. Will she ever want to meet me?'

'I'm sorry. I don't know her well enough to guess. Did Dot ever ask you to sell any artifacts for her?'

His brow furrowed.

'What sort of artefacts?'

'I thought you knew Flic practiced witchcraft?'

'I knew she believed in that stuff. She used to go to meetings with other people who followed Wicca. I didn't interfere. She was very spiritual. She used to collect herbs, and stones and little statues. I used to tease her, but she didn't like it.'

'Did she ever show you the antique items she guarded for the coven?'

'Never. But now that you mention it, I remember she kept them locked up, worried Dot might sell them.'

'But wasn't Dot a witch too?'

He snorted.

'Dot was as spiritual as a brick. She had no interest in ceremonies or rituals. She had a gambling habit which had led her to desperate measures to save her house. When she started running the fairs, she pulled herself back from the brink, but I heard she sold off some of the coven's property and replaced it with forgeries.'

'Where did you hear that?'

'I'm not at liberty to tell you.'

He smirked, and I recognised my phrase being used against me. Harry agreed with Roy over the price of the box and they shook hands over it. As we were leaving, Roy tapped me on the shoulder.

'Have you talked to Jasper Christie yet?'

'No. Should I?'

'He's not who he says he is, you know. There's more to him than meets the eye. I heard he had an arrangement with Dot. He wouldn't have taken it well if she reneged on it. He's a nasty little sod.'

The way he said it made me shiver. I already felt a little shell-shocked at the revelations about the sisters' past lives. I mulled over our conversation with Roy all the way home. He seemed like rather a loose cannon to me. His emotions when talking about the sisters had seemed raw, especially when it came to Felicity. He could be dangerous in the right situation, but would he have killed Dot? And why now? Harry left me to think. He always knows when I need space. He's the perfect boyfriend.

We bought Chinese takeaway on the way home from Mr Chen down at the harbour. He had bought new paper lanterns for the tiny restaurant and he beamed when I complimented him on them and gave me a fortune cookie. I broke it open and read the piece of a paper.

'Your confusion will be resolved.'

I hoped so. The tale of the two sisters had wormed its way under my skin. Whoever had murdered them had better watch out.

Chapter 17

The revelations about Roy and his relationships with the sisters had not removed him from the list of suspects. If anything, it made him more of a priority. Neither had Miles exonerated himself; if anything, his festering resentment topped Roy's. Dot had set herself to be murdered by anyone of half a dozen prime suspects. I couldn't separate them. After what Roy had said, Jasper Christie had to be added to the list as well. And then there was Abigail. I had to admit that she had a motive. Even if she was mistaken about Dot murdering her mother, Dot was responsible for her unhappiness.

Harry received a call from Sir Dudley proposing a visit to Cissbury Ring, complete with a picnic lunch. I invited Abigail too, as she had expressed an interest in a trip. Sir Dudley had been tongue-tied in her presence, and I wondered if I could do some good by encouraging their relationship. Abigail had shown no interest in Dudley, but she had been distressed and distracted at the funeral, as was to be expected. I called her without being sure of her reaction, but she accepted with alacrity.

'What a great idea! Sir Dudley? No, we don't really know each other, but I'm game.'

Sir Dudley insisted on being in charge of the picnic, which rankled with Harry who prided himself on his meticulous planning skills. Mrs Potts would not hear of Harry being involved either, so he backed down, muttering to himself. Given the recent heavy rainstorms, I had reservations about the wisdom of dining alfresco, but I chose not to voice them. Luckily, the weather seemed set fair as we left the Grotty Hovel. Mouse had a ferocious hangover and could not be persuaded to come with us. He had been hanging out with his old crowd, which worried me, but I hadn't approached the subject yet. He needed to make decisions about his future, but he showed no interest. Harry told me to give Mouse space, but I thought he needed direction. Add to that George's mounting impatience with his son, and I could see a flash point building up in front of us.

Soon, the fresh green leaves bursting from the branches along our route distracted me from my worries about Mouse, and I looked forward to our picnic instead. Even though it only took half an hour to drive there, I had never been to visit the Cissbury Ring before. I had friends who lived in London who had never been to visit the Tower of London. I guess we all think we'll get around to visiting the local sites, but are more likely to have been to the Colosseum in Rome, or the Acropolis in Athens, than the local museum. Harry whistled as we drove along, always a good sign with him. Despite obvious differences in their background, Harry had taken to Dudley, and vice-versa, over their love of military history.

I couldn't wait to get out in the fresh air and hear the birds singing without the herring gulls drowning them out with their squawking. Hades did a good job of massacring the local sparrow population, which did not go down well with me. He also killed dozens of mice, so I had to take the rough with the smooth. As we drew into the Storrington Rise car park from where we would walk to the fortifications, I spotted Abigail and Dudley chatting together. I crossed my fingers that they were finding things in common. Two lonely people might just solve each other's problem. I hadn't had much luck as a matchmaker for Ghita, but maybe this time I had managed a connection.

Dudley's housekeeper had loaded our picnic into some old-fashioned canvas rucksacks which Dudley and Harry carried between them, stating it was 'men's work'. I'm not stupid. I'll never stop a man carrying something if he wants to. It makes them feel macho and gives them purpose, so I said thank you. I noticed Abigail had worn a pair of heels, not high, but not great for walking. I had a spare pair of trainers in the car, but I didn't want to embarrass her by offering them. She had made an effort with her outfit, wearing a blue flowery dress with a lacy neckline and matching blue eyeshadow. From the way Dudley gazed at her, I thought she had hit the nail on the head. My more prosaic outfit of suede jacket and jeans looked a little dowdy in comparison, especially as I had matched it with walking boots, not knowing what to expect. I'm sure Abigail had her own opinions on my get-up.

We set out up the grassy path, which was dry and mud free.

Dudley took the lead, his plump cheeks wobbling as he almost bounded along the path. His joy at our excursion infected everyone. I grinned at him and enjoying the fresh air and buzzing of the bees. Early season meadow-brown and marble-white butterflies hovered above the tall grass, settling on wild flowers scattered within. Abigail collected a bunch of blooms and exclaimed with delight every time she found a new species to add. Harry looked around and winked at me. I hoped the picnic would not disappoint. I suspected Dudley had pulled out all the stops to impress us, his new friends. Sometimes a day will sit in your memory as perfect in every way. There were a couple in my past that I treasured and dwelled on to make me happy. I hoped this might be another one of them.

We reached the first kissing gate and followed the path along the edge of a copse of sycamore trees. Crossing another stile, the path led through a field of grass and another kissing gate which marked the entrance to the Cissbury Ring with a bench. We turned right under the ramparts and entered an area cratered like the moon's surface and covered with bushes and brambles. Footpaths snaked through the bushes and thick undergrowth and up onto the plateau that formed the bulk of the fort.

'These are the old flint mines,' said Dudley. 'They dug tunnels under the hill in Neolithic times. You might find a piece if you're lucky. Victorian archaeologists found axe heads here, which are now on display in the Seacastle Museum.'

We spend a good while searching the area for something more exciting than the discarded pieces of flint scattered around. Admitting defeat, we entered the ring through a gap in the Iron Age rampart up the slope onto the flat grassy knoll which sloped upwards to the northeast. More thick scrub and bushes were punctuated by clearings which offered panoramic views of the whole county. As I had suspected, Abigail found it pretty hard going in her heels, so I offered to sit with her on a lone bench, while the other two did a tour of the fortifications and the damage done during the Second World War. I would have liked to hear about it too, but getting Abigail on her own gave me a good chance to ask her a few questions about her relationship with Dot. We sat in the weak sunlight looking out over the channel past golden fields of barley and thick hedgerows vibrant with life. I could imagine why the mound had proved perfect as a fort, with its panoramic views of the surrounding countryside. Abigail examined her now wilting bunch of flowers.

'I should have left them growing,' she said. 'They were quite happy in the grass.'

Her bottom lip quivered.

'How are you holding up?' I asked. 'The house must be silent with Dot gone.'

'It's quite spooky, what with all her weird collection of magic artifacts.'

'How much do you know about them?'

'Just that they're about a million years old and belong to the club.'

'The club?'

'Yes, Dot belonged to some sort of magic club. She wouldn't tell me about it.'

So, Miles had not yet had his little chat with her. I couldn't be the first to break the news. I reversed.

'What will happen to the fair now Dot is gone? Will somebody else take over?'

'I'm not sure. There's a board of directors who manage the hall and decide on who can use it. I'm sure they want it to continue.'

'Did Dot own the rights to the fair?'

'I don't know. I'm sorry. She didn't tell me anything to tell you the truth. She treated me like a baby.'

'But you're an intelligent young woman. Maybe it's time you found out?'

She turned to look at me, blinking. It made me uncomfortable, as if she could see right through my platitudes. Then she laughed.

'Maybe it is. I've applied to find out the identity of my father, you know. I think it's time we met, even though Dot used to tell me horrible things about him. I need to judge for myself.'

'You might be surprised. Do you remember what you told me at the funeral? About Dot killing your mother.'

'Yes, I'm sorry to burden you like that. It's none of your business.'

'It might be important. I've been doing some investigating about your mother's fatal car crash and I think the two deaths may be linked.'

Abigail's face became pale as flour.

'Linked? But how?'

'I'm not sure yet. May I ask you a few questions?'

'Of course.'

Her fingers interlaced and her knuckles became white with tension.

'Why do you think Dot murdered your mother?'

'She hated her with a passion. I never found out why. I think it had something to do with my father.'

'So why did she take you on when your mother died? She didn't strike me as somebody who wanted children.'

'She didn't. I guess she did it out of loyalty to our family ties. In a way, I'm quite grateful. I would have had to go into a home otherwise. I suspect that would have been worse, but I never wanted to find out.'

I realised I had to tell her something about the accident or the poor girl would have that hate gnawing away inside with no way of relieving it.

'I've discovered something that may change your entire view of your mother's death, but I haven't confirmed it yet. Would you prefer me to tell you when I'm certain?'

'What sort of thing?'

'There was no car seat found at the scene of the accident. Why would someone have removed it before the accident, but then rescued you from the car afterwards, if they intended for you to be harmed? And how did Dot go about sabotaging the car? It's not like she had an aptitude for mechanics. It makes little sense.'

She stood up, her face bright red with emotion.

'You're trying to trick me,' she said.

'I would never lie about something so important.'

Abigail walked away from me and stared out across the downs. I could see her shoulders heaving. A flock of rooks flew overhead, calling to each other and heading for a ploughed field south of the fort. Time stood still as I waited. Had I done the wrong thing? She sat down again.

'You mean the cause of my mother's death is uncertain?'

'That's exactly what I mean, and I'm going to find out the truth. You have a right to know what happened that night. It may help you release some of your anger towards Dot. I doubt she sabotaged your mother's car, though. And she brought you up, even if she did a rotten job of it.'

'I can't believe it. All those years hating her and fighting her, and she may be innocent. It's an awful lot to take in. Can you keep me posted?'

'If you'd like.'

'Shh. The others are coming back. Can we keep this between ourselves? Sir Dudley would be so upset if we ruined his picnic.'

'Are you sure you'll be okay?'

'Yes. I don't know why, but I feel a lot better now.'

She stood up and went to meet the others. I felt guilty for telling her at that golden moment, but maybe her heart could heal with that knowledge, and it would be a gift.

Chapter 18

When we got home after our day out, Mouse greeted us at the door. His grey face told me all I needed to know about the sort of day he'd had. I almost felt sorry for him. Harry ruffled his hair.

'Still feeling rough?' he said. 'You need to lay off the booze.'

Mouse pulled away, frowning and restyled his hair in the mirror. He could be vain about his black curls.

'My head ached, but my brains were still working. I've been busy while you two were gallivanting about with the lords and ladies of the parish.'

'Really? I'm impressed. What have you been researching?' I asked.

'You know I've been trying to track down Jasper Christie? Well, he doesn't exist, not under that name anyway.'

'What do you mean?'

Mouse avoided my inquiring glance.

'If I tell you, will you promise not to get annoyed?'

'I have a feeling that's going to be tricky, but I'll do my best.'

'Let's all have a cup of tea first,' Harry suggested, heading for the kitchen. 'I'm parched.'

Hades yowled from his basket.

'We need to feed the monster too, by the sounds of it.' I said.

'Don't feed him anymore. He's been eating all day long. I'm surprised he hasn't burst at the seams,' said Mouse.

I filled the kettle and Harry got out the mugs and put milk and sugar on the table. Soon we were all seated with steaming cups of tea, handing round the chocolate digestives. I waited for Mouse to reveal his secret, but he seemed reluctant to speak.

'Are you going to tell us about Christie or not?' I asked.

Mouse sighed. 'I know you don't like him, but Fergal hung out with us last night.'

'Fergal? That tea leaf,' said Harry. 'You should pick your friends more carefully.'

'He wasn't invited, but he came over and joined us anyway. Some lads don't mind him.'

Mouse took a big slurp of tea.

'Anyway, I got talking with him after a couple of pints, and he pointed out this well-dressed bloke who he spotted standing at the bar. He told me the bloke came from a long line of forgers and swindlers. Apparently, he's notorious.'

'What's his name?'

'Cyril Wender. But he uses another name when he's working.'

'What name?' I asked, but I knew what he would say.

'Jasper Christie.'

Harry slapped his thigh and grinned at me.

'He's the bloke who tried to swindle you out of your table, isn't he?'

'The same. And Veronica Higgins told me he gave her an athame to sell at the fair. She said somebody stole it from their table while she and her husband went for coffee.'

'Maybe he changed his mind and took it back. Could that be the one used to murder Dot?'

'I don't know, but she told me it had some sort of snake on the hilt. I'll ask Flo if she'll send me a photograph of the complete knife. Mine is not at all clear.'

'Hardly surprising since it was embedded in the victim,' said Mouse.

I texted Flo with little hope, but she rang me almost immediately.

'Is this anything to do with the car crash? D.I. Antrim's been here talking to George.'

'I don't know yet, but it may be.'

'There's no harm in sending you a photo. George is planning on releasing it to the press anyway. It's so unusual we think it may be easy to trace back to its owner. I've got to go now. I have a report due in the morning. I'll drop into the Vintage for coffee next week.'

'Mouse is sending you a big hug.'

'He can give it to me in person when I come to the shop.'

She sent me the photographs shortly afterwards. Mouse put them up on his large screen and we all crowded around to have a look.

'Those aren't snakes,' said Harry. 'They're dragons.'

'How weird. Why would a coven in England have an athame with dragon carving on it? I might show this to Grace. Her shop is full of them. Maybe she'll know the significance.'

Chapter 19

The next morning, I went straight to visit Grace at her shop. She welcomed me in and made me a jasmine tea. I noticed dark circles under her eyes and she seemed nervous. I wondered if finding Dot's body haunted her more than she had admitted.

'What brings you here?' Grace said. 'I bet it's a development in the case. You're like Sherlock Holmes.'

'I don't know where to start, to tell the truth, but maybe you can help me.'

I flipped through the photographs on my cell phone until I found the one with the enlargement of the knife hilt. I passed it to Grace.

'Does this mean anything to you?' I asked.

To my surprise, she gasped and dropped the phone on the table, her face white. She appeared to be hyperventilating with shock. I couldn't think what to do. I reached out and touched her hand.

'Grace? Are you okay?'

She turned her face to me again. Her eyes were wide.

'I couldn't see it properly, you know,' she said.

'Shall I show you again?'

'No. Not that one. The other one.'

'I don't understand.'

'When I found her dead. I tried to examine the dagger, but the storage area was dark.'

'Were you doing that when I found you?'

'Yes.'

She looked at the photograph again.

'But why?'

Grace shrugged, her breathing returning to normal now. Colour returned to her cheeks too.

'Dot told me she possessed a historic Chinese dagger with dragons on the hilt, and offered to show it to me early that morning with a view of selling it to me. Dragons are special in our culture and, from her description, I believed it to be one of an ancient set of daggers missing for over a century. They disappeared during the Second Opium War when a regiment of British soldiers were billeted in Kowloon near the museum where they were kept. They were associated with business prosperity, bountiful harvests, good health and protection. I have a client who would pay a fortune for any of these artefacts. He would pay more for a set.'

'Is it the real thing?'

'I can't tell in a photograph. I'd need to see it up close. Why?'

'I need to know if it's a forgery.'

'A forgery? But why would she try to sell me a fake dagger? She would have known it wasn't original.'

'Perhaps. Or maybe she had been conned.'

'Conned? By who?'

'I have my suspicions. Would you come to the station and examine the dagger for me?'

'The police station? I'm not sure I'm brave enough.'

'I'll be with you. George will be grateful for the help. Perhaps you'll be a witness instead of a suspect this time?'

I couldn't suppress a smirk. Grace pouted.

'You are not a serious person,' she said. 'I should not help you.'

'But you will?'

'If it helps find Dot's murderer, I will help.'

We walked the short distance to the police station. I took Grace's arm to show solidarity and also to stop her from running off again. The entire episode has changed my perception of her as cool and unruffled by anything. Instead, she resembled a swan, serene on the surface, but paddling away like fury out of sight. I pushed open the door of the reception, relieved to note that no one else waited in the reception. Sally Wright, the police receptionist, raised an eyebrow when I entered the station with Grace.

'You're brave,' she said. 'George is looking for you.'

'He's not much of a detective then; he's got my cell phone number.'

'Shall I tell him you're here?'

'We want to see Flo. Can you buzz us through?'

'Is she expecting you? She's rushed off her feet.'

'It won't take more than five minutes of her time.'

'I'll need to ask George first.'

The stubborn look on her face gave us no quarter.

'Okay.'

She rang his extension and told him we were in reception. Whatever he said made her bite her lip in amusement.

'He'll be out,' she said.

Grace tugged at my arm and I knew she had changed her mind, but I ignored her. I patted her arm and smiled at her.

'I'll deal with George. You speak to Flo.'

The inner door swung outwards and George held it open for us to enter.

'So good of you to pop in,' he said. 'You must be psychic.'

'No problem,' I said. 'Is it okay that Grace goes through to have a word with Flo while we talk?'

He shook his head.

'I think Grace needs to speak to me too. Why don't you ladies come into the interview room with me?'

Sweat had broken out on Grace's forehead. George put a firm hand on the small of her back and guided her into the interview room. I took off my shoes, mindful of the electric shocks I usually got from the metal chair on the nylon carpet. George tutted.

'Do you have to do that, Tan?'

I ignored him and sat down beside Grace, who had the air of somebody waiting for the executioner to arrive. It appeared her experience of the police in Hong Kong had left her traumatised. She flashed me a look of panic. I patted her knee and gave her a reassuring smile.

'D.I. Antrim came to see me yesterday,' said George, drumming his fingers on the table.

'That's nice,' I said. 'Was it a social visit?'

'He wanted to talk to me about a car accident that happened twenty years ago.'

'He's an odd sort of fellow.'

'And you know nothing about this?'

'About what?'

George sighed, a long, exasperated sound.

'Have you been talking to D.I. Antrim?' he said.

'Is that illegal?'

George let out a deep breath and addressed Grace instead of me.

'Honestly, Grace, I don't know how you can stand it. Do you know anything about this?'

She glanced at me, and I notice her lips curl into a tiny smile as she joined me in my game.

'About what?'

I smothered a guffaw, and, beside me, Grace was wide eyed at her own courage. George turned back to me and folded his arms.

'D.I. Antrim thinks the two cases are linked, and he wants us to work together on them,' he said. 'Why would he develop an interest in a car accident from twenty years ago?'

'Aren't the two women sisters?' I asked.

'But how did he know that?'

'I expect he interviewed Dot when Felicity died.'

'How did you know I was talking about that accident?'

Damn! I put my hands up.

'Okay. You got me. Abigail Nash asked me to look into the death of her mother, Felicity. Then Miles Quirk came by Grace's shop to buy a plate and he mentioned that D.I. Antrim had been the policeman on site at the accident.'

'He just mentioned it in conversation about a plate?'

'I may have asked him a couple of questions about it. I don't know why you're annoyed. I'm not interfering in your case, I'm interfering in D.I. Antrim's case.'

I heard a snort beside me. Grace pretended to blow her nose, her shoulders shaking. George closed his eyes and swallowed.

'I hear you want to see Flo? What about?'

'Grace thinks she can identify the origin of the dagger. Would that help your inquiry?'

'It might. Would it help yours?'

'They may be linked.'

'I can see where this is going,' said George, wiping his brow. 'Come on. I'll take you both to see Flo.'

He stood up and pushed my shoes towards me with his foot. I put them back on and we passed through the office under the bemused glances of George's team. PC Joe Brennan gave me a wink, which his boss did not spot. We descended to Flo's empire and knocked on the door of her office. She answered almost immediately, her dark hair with its badger stripe of grey piled on her head in a rebellious castle. She had a spotless lab coat on and safety glasses perched on the top of her head.

'A delegation?' she said. 'What fun! How can I help?'

'We've come to see the dagger,' said Grace.

'Grace thinks she can identify its origins,' I said.

'It could help us solve Dot's murder, or even link two murders if we are lucky,' said George. 'Please can you put it out on a tray for us so Grace can inspect it. She'll need gloves, a face mask and a hairnet to avoid contaminating it. Perhaps a disposable lab coat too?'

Once Grace had been kitted up, and the protocols signed and chain of evidence noted, Flo put the knife in a spotless metal tray and Grace leaned over it with a large magnifying glass. She nodded and muttered to herself several times before straightening and turning to us.

'This dagger is a copy,' she said. 'But they must have copied the original to produce such an accurate fake.'

'A copy?' said George. 'Of what?'

'The original set of Dragon Knives disappeared during the Second Opium War. They were a sacred relic owned by a powerful family in Hong Kong. The British looted them, but they disappeared and were never seen again after 1862.'

'Why is that important?' said Flo.

'Because they are priceless,' said Grace.

'And if someone tried to sell a fake to somebody who realised it was a copy, might they be enraged?' said George.

The room echoed with his question. Grace peeled off her gloves and dropped them in the bin at her feet.

'Are you asking me if I killed Dot in a fit of rage?' she said.

'You seem to be the only one who knew their value,' said George.

'Dot and the forger knew,' I said. 'And anyone who is holding one or the rest of the set. We need to find out how they arrived in England, and where they've been hiding for the last century and a half.'

'Since Grace can recognise the originals, it might be an idea if she worked with us on this case,' said George. 'But, as a person of interest, she has to be supervised. I can't believe I'm saying this, but will you offer your services to the police, Tan? We can pay you as a consultant. Not much, but something.'

'What would you like us to do?'

'Can you start by researching the history of the knives? Who brought them here and what happened to them since? You must alert me at the first sign of danger. Grace can identify any daggers you discover. How does that sound?'

I felt a beam spread over my features. Grace's eyes were shining with excitement. She nodded at me. I turned back to George.

'Where do we sign?'

Chapter 20

My investigation took on a new impetus with the revelation that the original dagger, on which the forged one used to kill Dorothy Parker-Styles was based, belonged to a historically significant set removed from Hong Kong during the Second Opium War. Veronica Higgins, having had her husband returned by the police, showed no inclination to pay for my services, but I didn't mind. I had the bit between my teeth and my investigative training had kicked in. And we were getting a stipend from the police for consulting too. Quite a turn up for the books, as Harry said.

While I composed lists of suspects and motives, Mouse sat with me combing through the internet for references to the Dragon Daggers. His fingers flew over the keys, distracting me from my work. I had mastered search engines, but Mouse had skills I could only dream of. Hades did his utmost to disrupt proceedings by lying along the keyboard, but Mouse tipped him off without ceremony. Hades gave us both black looks and slunk out to the bramble patch to massacre any wildlife still standing. He thought he ruled the roost at the Grotty Hovel and couldn't believe it when his humans rebelled.

Mouse soon confirmed that the Queen's Royal Regiment was stationed at Kowloon during the War. He found an archive listing all the men who served in the regiment and separated out those who served between

1840 and 1870. Then he searched for familiar names among the officers stationed there. From the depth of the sighs he issued, I gathered reviewing lists of enlisted men and officers did not thrill him as much as it might. I made the task less onerous by getting him to print out some of them and helping with the search. We ate tomato soup and cheese on toast for lunch, which cheered us both up and gave us fresh enthusiasm for the task. The lists were in alphabetical order and I soon progressed to the surnames beginning with S. It didn't take me long to spot a name I recognised.

'Oh my goodness,' I said. 'You'll never guess what.'

Mouse spun his chair to face me.

'Tell me,' he said. 'I need good news.'

'There's a Brigadier John Seagrove listed here as posted to Hong Kong.'

'Why is he our man?'

'Sir Dudley Seagrove told us his mother played at being a witch. What if she belonged to the same hereditary coven as Dot? Perhaps the Dragon daggers were distributed between the members of the Seacastle coven by Brigadier Seagrove or a descendant of his?'

'But how do you know he's a relative of Sir Dudley's?'

'I don't, but while we were in Dudley's house, I noticed various portraits of military types hanging in the stairwell. We were discussing antiques, so I didn't notice who they were, or which regiment.'

'I'll look him up.'

He spun back to the computer and put his head down again, his keyboard clattering. A series of tuts and mutters followed. Then a crow of triumph.

'Ah, here he is. Apparently, Brigadier Seagrove went to Hong Kong in 1861 and came back three years later. He brought a great deal of booty back with him, which he declared to the state. Amongst the items, he mentioned a set of six daggers decorated with dragons.'

'Can you find a family tree for the Seagroves of Sussex? It would be useful to know where Dudley comes in.'

'Give me a minute. I'll open the Burke's Peerage website.'

I looked over his shoulder as he waded through pages of landed gentry until he found the correct Seagroves.

'There you go,' he said. 'Dudley is a direct descendant of Brigadier Seagrove.'

'Meaning he would have inherited the daggers if the family still had them. Going by the state of his house, he would sell them if he knew their value. I saw rising damp in the hallway.'

'But if they belong to the Seagroves, how did somebody get their hands on one of them? I mean, I know the dagger used to stab Dot was a forgery, but whoever made it needed to copy the original.'

'How would we find out?'

'Sir Dudley is the one to ask. He didn't seem too interested in witchcraft or magic, but he's a history buff. I'm sure he'll know something.'

'Didn't you see a witch in Brighton?' said Mouse. 'Surely, she knows something about the history of the coven?'

'That's a brilliant suggestion! Perpetua had volumes of what looked like records for the coven stored in her kitchen. Maybe we'll ask Dudley first, though. You never know what records are stored in that extensive library he had in his house. Harry and I will get it all out of him if we can.'

As I had expected, Sir Dudley agreed to have us over for a drink and a browse through the library when we asked him for permission. He seemed bemused that one of his ancestors might have something to do with Dot's demise, but I promised to explain all when we arrived. My sister Helen offered to drop us off at the house, so we could have a couple of drinks and then take a taxi home, without worrying about being over the limit for driving. I couldn't help feeling excited on our way there. Helen, in her self-imposed role as the sensible sister tried to damp down my mood.

'Do you imagine Sir Dudley will show you proof his ancestor stole precious artefacts from Hong Kong? There's no way you'll get anywhere with him. George is relying on you for once. Don't let him down, or I'll have to put up with his complaints about you.'

'It will be interesting,' said Harry. 'No matter what. And I hear Sir Dud has a magnificent cellar full of lovely red wine.'

'Hmm. It doesn't sound like work to me,' said Helen, pursing her lips.

'It's good of you to give us a lift,' I interjected, eager to change the subject. 'We don't see you often enough these days. Promise you'll come to supper when Olivia is back from university?'

'That would be nice. And we haven't fed Herbert for ages either. The weather has been atrocious.'

We were on safer ground with weather and children. Helen took a dim view of me investigating crimes allocated to her boyfriend. They were two peas in a pod. I thought they should get married so they could whinge about me and the weather into their dotage. George would be off my hands forever if he married my sister. I hadn't an ounce of jealousy towards them, only astonishment that he had married me first. Second time lucky is a thing.

Sir Dudley came out to greet us at the front door of his house and declared himself enraptured with Helen. Her matronly air of combined reward and punishment appealed to most public-school graduates. They gravitated to her like worker bees around a queen. He even tried to persuade her to stay and received a quick lecture on the perils of drink driving which sent him close to ecstasy. After she left, he stood gazing at the departing car and muttered 'remarkable woman' under his breath before ushering us into the library.

'Do you mind if I use your bathroom?' said Harry. 'Too much tea as usual.'

'It's under the staircase. Mind your head as you go in.'

I followed Sir Dudley into the library, which smelled of old paper and stale cigar smoke. A tray with the ingredients for gin and tonics perched on a gate-legged table in the alcove under one of the large windows. The centre of the room contained battered leather sofas and chairs with patches which attempted to stem the escape of their emerging stuffing. When Harry came back from the toilet, Sir Dudley poured us all a stiff drink and we sat opposite him on the sofa. He occupied a chair which seemed to be his favourite, from the way he patted its arms as if it were a dog.

'What's this all about?' he said. 'I enjoy a good mystery.'

'Dot Parker-Styles was stabbed with a copy of one of a set of historical daggers,' I said. 'Our friend Grace, the one who discovered Dot's body, told us that the originals would be priceless if found.'

Sir Dudley shifted in his seat and took a slug of his drink.

'What has that got to do with me?'

'We've discovered that an ancestor of yours was stationed in Kowloon during the Second Opium War,' said Harry. 'And he left Hong Kong carrying these daggers with him.'

'An ancestor of mine? I don't think so. I'd know if any such person existed.'

'Mouse looked him up in Burke's peerage,' I said. 'You're directly descended from him.'

Sir Dudley deflated.

'We think somebody got hold of one of those daggers and copied it,' said Harry. 'And then we remembered that your mother used to hang around with Dot and the other witches.'

'She did, but I never took it seriously.'

'Did she keep any witchcraft paraphernalia at home?' said Harry. 'Maybe she kept the daggers hidden from you. It's likely she did not know their value.'

'I found a box of weird stuff, but I put it in the attic. We can take it down from there if you like.'

'Can I help?' said Harry.

'No thanks. It's like Aladdin's cave up there, and inches thick in dust. I'm the only one who knows where everything is. Give me a few minutes and I'll bring it down to you.'

He drained his glass and heaved himself to standing.

'I'll be back shortly,' he said.

When Dudley had gone, I turned to Harry.

'I don't think he was being truthful with us.'

'He isn't. I nipped upstairs for a butcher's at the family portraits. There's one of someone called Brigadier John Seagrove hanging above the bathroom.'

'But why would he lie?'

'Maybe he's ashamed of the looting that went on. I expect the Chinese would be keen to get their daggers back too. He may want to keep them secret. The sink in the toilet is broken, which adds to the general impression of decay around here. Perhaps Dot wasn't the only person who wanted to sell their dagger.'

'I think we need to visit Perpetua and her history books.'

'Who's that then?' said Sir Dudley, coming back into the library.

'Oh, just a friend of ours who may have known your mother. Didn't you find the box?'

'It's dashed strange, but I couldn't spot it anywhere. I'll have to look for it again in the daylight.'

'That is odd,' said Harry. 'But I spend my life crawling around amongst other people's belongings. It's easy to misplace a box, or even forget one. It'll turn up.'

'If I refill your glasses, will you tell me about your best finds on the job? It sounds so fascinating.'

Harry elbowed me in the ribs.

'Why don't you tell him about the taxidermy fish?'

Chapter 21

Perpetua Hastings greeted us with a distinct lack of enthusiasm when we returned to her shop in Brighton. The sign board outside announced a special offer of three for two on herbal sachets. Perpetua, who had dressed in a voluminous purple floor-length dress with a plunging neckline, gestured at it.

'All witches are bargain hunters,' she said. 'I suppose trying to get something for nothing sums up witchcraft to some extent.'

I couldn't tell if she meant it as a joke or not, so I half smiled. Grace started sorting through the sachets as soon as we got inside. She can't resist a bargain.

'I wasn't expecting to see you two ladies again so soon,' said Perpetua. 'What can I do for you this time?'

'We've been doing research on the dagger used to kill Dot. It turns out to be one of a set of six taken from Hong Kong in the nineteenth century. I wondered if you could let us go through the record books to find the first mention of the daggers. Also, it's important we find out the names of the families who received them.'

'What's so important about the daggers?' said Perpetua.

'The complete set would be almost priceless,' Grace said. 'But the individual daggers are also valuable antiques. It may be a motive for Dot's murder.'

'Somebody killed her for the dagger? But why did they leave it in the body?' said Perpetua.

'The one used to stab Dot was a forgery. Perhaps the killer took the original but left the forgery to confuse the police?' said Grace.

Perpetua blinked and held on to the edge of the cash desk for a second.

'A forgery? How can you be sure?'

'The police showed it to me,' said Grace. 'I'm from Hong Kong and I have thirty years' experience as an antique dealer over there. That's why I'm helping on the case.'

'The police hired us to help them find the murderer by following the trail left by the daggers,' I said. 'Anyway, we need to find out who received the originals, as they may be in danger.'

Perpetua pouted.

'These books are sacred relics only to be read by members of the coven. I can't let you have them.'

'But you can read them for us. All we need is a list of names of the families who hold the daggers now.'

Perpetua pushed her way through the beaded curtain into the kitchen. She did not offer us tea this time. Her rigid back told me all I needed to know about her resistance to this plan. I suspected she didn't need to look up any of the information surrounding the daggers, but I went with it. Grace pulled up a chair and pretended to examine the herbal sachets she had selected. Perpetua ran her finger along the historical records, reading the years out loud.

'Here we are,' said Perpetua. 'This book covers the second half of the twentieth century.'

She pulled it from the shelf above, dislodging a host of dead flies and cobwebs. Perpetua wound the web and its crispy occupants around a pencil and stuck it in a jar without comment. I guessed it might be used in one of her spells or potions, though I didn't dare ask. She brushed the dust off the book with a feather duster, causing Grace to sneeze several times. Then she took a wand out of her dress pocket and muttered an incantation over the book. I half expected invisible forces to open it to the correct page. The muttering went on for a long time. Grace raised an eyebrow at me, but I waited.

Perpetua sighed and opened the book on the first page. The pages had been loosely bound and were of differing sizes and thickness. I tried to read them upside down from where I sat, but witches and doctors had similar handwriting. Most of them were almost hieroglyphical in style with a myriad of odd symbols substituting for words. To my relief, Perpetua had ceased to procrastinate and flipped through the pages at a decent rate.

'Let me see. Ah, here we are. Have you got a pen?'

I had, but of course it wouldn't write. I scrabbled in my handbag for a second one, finding only an ancient green biro at the bottom. Since it wrote smoothly, I didn't wonder where it came from, but held it above my notebook, ready for action.

'In 1970, the Seacastle coven broke off from the New Forest coven, led by Lady Agnes Seagrove. She invited six families to join the coven and presented each of the couples with a dragon dagger. The names of the families are Hastings, Seagrove, Parker-Styles, Quirk, Farnham and Taylor.'

'Sir Dudley's family had one? Why didn't he say so?' I asked.

'Maybe he didn't know. We keep them hidden from non-Wicca persons; you know.'

'But isn't Sir Dudley the heir to his mother's place in the coven?'

'In theory, but he has no interest in keeping up with tradition. He possesses no spirituality or contact with the earth.'

'And Miles had one too? He didn't mention it either.'

Perpetua shrugged.

'That's hardly suspicious behaviour. It's his duty to be discreet. An ancient athame has immense power if it falls into the wrong hands, you know.'

'What sort of power?' said Grace, but Perpetua ignored her.

'Who holds the daggers now?' I asked.

'It's a hereditary coven. The daggers have passed down from generation to generation in the same families. Lady Seagrove had one and Dot had another. They used to spend a lot of time together you know. Then there's Miles Quirk and myself. The other two reside with the Farnham and Taylor families.'

'Aren't you worried people will sell them now that they're worth so much?'

Perpetua tutted.

'We don't own the daggers. The coven does. We can't sell them or give them away, only give them back to the coven.'

'But Dot had offered to sell me hers,' said Grace. 'That's why I went to meet her.'

'She went too far, but that was always her problem. Look what happened to Felicity.'

'Do you believe Dot sabotaged Felicity's car?' I asked.

'I have no proof, but if Felicity hadn't died, Dot would have got nowhere near the daggers. I always suspected that Dot killed Felicity out of jealousy when Felicity had been elected coven leader and not her. On top of that, Dot thought Felicity had stolen Roy from her and had been stewing with hatred for years.'

'So, who killed Dot?' said Grace.

'I'd say cherchez la femme, but in this case, I'd go for revenge. I suspect Roy Loveday. He never got over Felicity's death. And then, of course, there's Miles. He's not half as diffident as he pretends to be. He hated Dot with a passion. If he discovered she was selling her dagger to the highest bidder, he might have snapped.'

'What about Abigail?' I asked. 'She hated Dot and believed her responsible for her mother's murder.'

'I find it hard to believe Abigail is capable of such a thing,' said Perpetua. 'She's as limp as a dishcloth.'

I didn't agree, but there didn't seem to be any point in debating it with her. We thanked her and made our way back to the car.

'I didn't know being a witch was so complicated,' said Grace.

On the way home, I telephoned George to update him on our progress. He had not spoken to Roy Loveday or Miles yet.

'I'll move them to the top of my suspects list and get them in for an interview. I can't believe I'm saying this, but have you tracked down the other witches yet?'

'There are two families we haven't come across before, but I'll get Mouse to research them.'

'Do you and Grace want to come along as observers?'

'Let me know where and when.'

Chapter 22

As expected, Jasper Christie had disappeared once he got wind of the police search for him. I suspected he had switched identities back to Cyril Wender again and fled. Instead, George and his team concentrated on bringing in Roy Loveday and Miles Quirk for questioning, but came up against a brick wall in their interviews.

'It's like trying to squeeze blood from a stone,' George told me. 'They've both clammed up tight. Neither of them pretended to have any affection for Dot, but they both claim to have alibis for the night of her death. Flo is awaiting forensic results from the dagger used to stab Dot, but we need reasonable ground for requesting a DNA sample from Loveday and Quirk. At the moment, we can't be sure either of them had anything to do with Dot's murder. There's a ton of motive on both sides, but no physical evidence. We couldn't hold either of them.'

Grace took a dim view of British policing now that they had dropped her as a suspect.

'These men hated Dot. Why can't the police arrest them and take their DNA? I don't understand.'

'The law protects everyone from wrongful arrest, even people from Hong Kong,' I said, earning a black look from her and a wink from Max.

'They'd soon talk if I was in charge,' said Grace.

Following confirmation from Perpetua on the names of those who held the daggers, Mouse had researched the

Farnham and Taylor families and discovered that both of them lived in the Lancing area. The Farnhams ran a dairy farm, and the Taylors had a chain of hardware stores in West Sussex. To my relief, both households remembered me from my former career on *Uncovering the Truth* and agreed to see me at the weekend to discuss the death of Dot Parker-Styles and the history of the Seacastle Coven. I told them I had been commissioned to write an article for the local paper and I would bring a photographer with me. Grace borrowed Max's Pentax and lenses for authenticity, but I doubted she knew how to use them. If either family still had their daggers, Grace would examine them to confirm their authenticity.

While I waited for the interviews, Harry secured the right to clear out a couple of shipping containers at the storage depot behind Sainsbury's. The owners of the contents had disappeared owing three months' rental, and the manager of the storage depot had received permission to empty the containers in order to hire them out to people who would pay. I couldn't wait to spend some time with Harry. Grace did not have a sense of humour and our music tastes were further apart than the stars in the Milky Way. Her razor-sharp intellect did not compensate for the gloom on our drives without loud music and bad jokes.

'I've been feeling neglected,' said Harry, as I jumped into the front seat of the van.

I took this as an invitation to give him a long and sloppy kiss while draping myself across the steering wheel. I gave the horn a sharp blast with my elbow, which brought us up short.

'Whatever will the neighbours think?' said Harry, beaming.

'That I've missed you loads and I love you even more.'

'Keep going. I'm going to need a lot more buttering up after being usurped by Grace Wong.'

'Don't be silly. She's the key to the investigation. She's the only one who can tell a real dagger from a forgery.'

'Um, about that, I've been thinking.'

'Tell me on the way to the storage centre.'

He started the engine and pulled out from the kerb. As we turned onto the main road, he stroked his chin.

'Well, if she's the only one who can tell if they are forgeries or not, couldn't she be lying about which dagger is valuable?'

'I suspect Miles Quirk can tell the difference between the real and the forged too, but you've made a good point. I still don't think she'd have stabbed Dot without keeping the dagger. It seems more like a message, leaving it there. They're pretty unique.'

'A message to who?'

'Ah. That I can't tell you.'

The manager of the storage facility met us outside the fence of the compound housing the shipping containers. He had a large four-wheeled trolley with a heavy-duty bolt cutter on it.

'You might need this to carry your booty,' he said. 'No vans are allowed inside the compound.'

We followed him down the rows of containers until he stopped and checked his clipboard.

'These two,' he said, and turned to pick up the bolt cutter.

He snipped through the locks on the doors like he was cutting spaghetti.

'There you go. Thanks for your custom.'

He held out his hand and Harry counted out two hundred pounds into it. As always, the risk of paying sight unseen for the contents of a shipping container made my hairs stand on end with anticipation. Most containers wiped their faces, but the occasional bust happened. People who could afford to hire a shipping container had something worth keeping in them, but sometimes they couldn't face getting rid of their mother's three-piece suite and bed, which should have been taken to the tip instead. Harry noticed my tense expression and laughed.

'It's like the Grand National, isn't it?'

He shook the first latch free of the destroyed lock and swung the door open. Lines of boxes piled three high filled the container. Harry pulled one out and opened it. He showed me a tin of tomatoes, shaking his head with disappointment.

'This is not our sort of container,' he said. 'What are we going to do with all this?'

'Maybe Rohan and Kieron need supplies?'

'For the restaurant that never opens? I doubt it, but why don't you give them a ring when we take an inventory?'

'What about the food bank?'

'Ah, now there's an idea. Let's ask Rohan first and give the rest to charity. At least we can get our money back.'

It took us over an hour to make an inventory of the boxes, all of which contained foodstuffs, either tinned or bagged dry goods. I called Rohan who offered to take some of it, but the food bank would be the principal beneficiary of our bounty. We moved over to the second container, less enthusiastic than we had been before.

'Go on,' I said. 'Open it.'

Harry undid the latch and opened the door to reveal nothing but empty space.

'Looks like we've been had,' he said.

'Or the storage manager has.'

I noticed an envelope taped to the wall of the container and pulled it off. I took a piece of paper out of it and skimmed the contents.

'What does it say?' said Harry.

'It claims the manager is having an affair with the wife of the person who's renting the container, so they purposely rented the unit without paying to teach him a lesson.'

'Seriously? What a pain. Do you think we should give the note to the manager?'

'Do you think he'll give us our money back?'

In the end, we took the note to the manager, who gave us half of our money back. It took us an age to load the van with the boxes of supplies and the rain fell as we finished up, which did not improve our moods. It was a relief to leave and set off home. I couldn't wait to get home and have a glass of wine on my sofa.

About five minutes after we set out for home, a loud bang made us both jump. Smoke issued from the bonnet and the van rolled to a halt at the side of the road. We sat there in silence for a moment, taking in the implications of the bang. I knew the inevitable had happened to our old work horse after many years of faithful service. Harry's face fell, and he shook his head.

'And I thought the day couldn't get any worse,' he said. 'But what did I know?'

We got out of the van and Harry opened the bonnet, letting out a cloud of acrid smoke. He wafted his hands over the engine, shaking his head. He pulled at some wires and jiggled the oil tester, but we both knew he was straightening the corpse's tie at a funeral.

'We'd better call the tow truck,' said Harry. 'We can't leave the old girl at the side of the road.'

I squeezed his hand.

'I'll look up the number.'

Chapter 23

When I got back to the Grotty Hovel, the place was deserted. Mouse had left several dirty cups in the sink and from the telltale smell of weed, his dodgy friends had paid him a visit. I imagined he had put this phase of his life behind him, but he had become bored with running the Vintage, and the small salary I could pay him. He tried to hide it, and helped me with my sleuthing without complaint if I asked him, but he needed more from life. George had tried to have a man-to-man talk with him, but had been met with derision. I sympathised. If a helicopter parent is annoying, a submarine parent who only surfaces when there is trouble, and then disappears again, is worse.

Our abortive trip to the storage depot had given me cause to worry about Harry too. His beloved van had over two hundred thousand miles on the clock and had been threatening to fail its next MOT. But the engine had expired with no hope of salvaging it. Harry's van was a family heirloom, inherited from his uncle, and chock full of sentimental value. He had driven up to the Grotty Hovel in the same van the first time I had met him and I could picture his burly frame emerging as if it were yesterday. Apart from anything else, I knew finances were tight; tighter now the containers had been useless. I wondered how we could buy another van with our finances in such a parlous state.

I noticed Mouse had left me a note which had fluttered to the floor when I opened the front door. His neat handwriting always surprised me with its elegant curves. He had left me instructions for getting to the Farnham and Taylor residences and a list of questions I could ask. He had a great curiosity and an analytical mind that was wasted in his present position. I had to find something interesting for him to study, even though he baulked at the thought of structured courses. But how to tell him what to do without appearing to tell him what to do? He would be twenty soon, and hopefully his teenage rebellion would be over then.

I poured myself a glass of wine and sat on the sofa with my feet up. Eyes closed, I tried to meditate, following an app on my phone. The soothing voice usually lulled me to sleep, but my agitation kept me awake. Trying to empty my mind turned out to be as easy as emptying a bath with a sieve. I tried to slow my breathing and had some success. Just when I felt quite smug and accomplished, my cell phone rang, making me jump and slosh some wine on the carpet. I had forgotten that I still clung to the glass like a sailor to a life raft. I grabbed the phone, thinking it might be Harry with news on the van, but I saw DI Antrim's number on the screen. My heart rate sped up again. Could he have news on our case?

'Hello,' I said.

I almost called him Terry, but he may not have appreciated it, our relationship being limited to work only.

'Ms Bowe,' he said. 'Are you busy? I've got some news. George and I are meeting in the Shanty to discuss the case if you fancy coming along?'

I checked my glass, which was still half full.

'Can you pick me up please? I've had half a glass of wine and I'm not sure if I'm over the limit for driving.'

'Of course. I'm only a couple of streets away.'

'How do you know where I live?'

I could hear the amusement in his voice when he answered.

'I'm a policeman. I know where everybody lives. Give me ten minutes.'

By the time my phone pinged at me, I had brushed my hair, put on some lipstick and changed my shirt for a clean tunic. I grabbed my coat from the stand and went out into the street. DI Antrim's car idled beside the pavement. I jumped in and put on my seatbelt.

'All set?' he said. 'George is already there. Text him your drink order.'

I could only imagine how George would react to me sending him instructions like that.

'I'll choose when I get there,' I said.

We left the car parked as close as possible to the pub and set off down the footpath towards the Shanty, which seemed even closer to the edge of the bluff. The sun had almost set, and the pub glowed golden in the last rays of sunlight. I ducked into the door and looked around to see George sitting at the bar chatting to Joy. He waved me over, and I kissed her on the cheek.

'Is Ryan around?' I asked.

'He's working,' said Joy.

I knew what that meant, but I just nodded.

'Can I have a soda and lime please?'

'Are you on a health kick,' said George. 'Put a gin in that, Joy. She'll need it.'

I wondered what revelation about the case would drive me to drink.

'I'll have a shandy, please,' said DI Antrim. 'Just a half.'

We took our drinks to the snug where we could talk with no one overhearing us. I sat beside George on the velvet banquette. It felt like old times coming to the pub to talk about a case in hushed tones with my erstwhile husband.

'We found the accident report for Felicity Nash's crash. It took us a week to dig up the file,' said DI Antrim. 'Somebody had put it in the wrong box. And then we had to find the witnesses. One paramedic had moved to Australia.'

He took a sip of his shandy and smacked his lips, looking around the snug.

'Shall I buy us some pork scratchings?' he said. 'I'm feeling peckish.'

I sighed, and George laughed.

'Come on, Terry. Spill the beans before Tan explodes.'

Terry Antrim smirked. I knew he had done it on purpose. George wasn't the only DI who like to wind me up.

'We got hold of everyone to review their findings from the case. We even got hold of the technician who examined the car for evidence of sabotage.'

'That's great news, isn't it?'

'Well, it is, and it isn't. There's a problem. One which sends the investigation back to the starting gate.'

'Which is?' I said.

George snorted.

'Patience, woman.'

I shot him a look, but he ignored me.

'There appears to have been some potential evidence of sabotage by piercing the brake lines, but it wasn't clear cut because of the fire. Also, there seemed to be zero motive to kill a young mother. So the judge ruled death by misadventure.'

DI Antrim took a long draught of his shandy.

'We don't have the car anymore, so we can't do more extensive testing. There is no way of getting a definitive answer. However, if someone hoped to cause an accident, they were not plotting to kill Felicity.'

'And how do you know that?' said George.

'Because the car which crashed belonged to Dot. A fact overlooked during the inquiry.'

I gasped in shock.

'But that means…'

'Different motives and different suspects. We need to start from zero.'

'And that will affect my case too,' said George. 'If the original motive has changed, the motive for the second murder will also have changed.'

I sat back stunned. What would Mouse make of this? Or Harry. Or Grace? I made frantic scribbles in my notebook. I could feel both men watching me. I looked up again.

'I'm sorry,' I said. 'But after the day I've had, there is nothing I can contribute right now.'

Chapter 24

The next morning, I awoke with a case of shell shock. After going back to square one, I felt like giving up my investigation. With two DIs on the job, my contribution would be minimal. But then I remembered I had appointments to interview the Farnhams and the Taylors. They might explain why Dot had been targeted twice over twenty years. I could believe somebody wanted her dead, but why the enormous time gap between attempts? Maybe two different people were involved. And who had the motive to kill Dot? Roy Loveday still seemed to be the prime suspect. Not only did he hate Dot, but he had experience working as a mechanic. Had he killed Felicity by mistake? Surely, he would have recognised Dot's car? Why had he waited so long to try again? Maybe the row about the table at the fair had pushed him over the edge, as I first suspected.

I showered and dressed, and got ready to collect Grace, trying to gee myself up to do the interviews. Before Dot's death, I did not know covens even existed anymore. I found it fascinating people still cast spells and hexes in the twenty-first century. Being holed up for years with depression had made me cynical about all things spiritual. I knew people had superstitions about crystals and spirits, but until I entered Perpetua's shop, I had imagined spells and incantations to be limited to fans of Harry Potter. As I left the Grotty Hovel, barring the door to Hades who tried to scamper past me, Harry sent me a text about his van which read 'She's gone for good. RIP to the old girl'. I felt the emotion behind his brief message and sent him condolences and kisses.

Grace stood outside her front door with Max's camera bag swinging from her shoulder. She had dressed in khaki, for some reason known only to herself, and she looked like a war correspondent.

'We're only going to West Sussex,' I said, as she got into the car.

'I'm getting into character,' she said, pouting.

'You look fab, though.'

She beamed.

'How far are we going?' she asked.

'Only twenty miles. We're seeing the Farnhams first and then the Taylors. We might have time for a pub lunch in between, depending on how it goes. By the way, I have news about the car accident that killed Felicity. You will not believe this, but it appears somebody targeted Dot and killed Felicity by mistake.'

'How did you work that out?'

'The car which crashed belonged to Dot. It seems Felicity drove off in Dot's car in a fit of pique, but somebody had interfered with the brake line earlier. Nobody on the investigating team noticed the car didn't belong to Felicity, and Dot told no one.'

'How weird. But it explains why she looked after Abigail. She must have felt responsible in some way.'

'But why did someone try to kill Dot?'

'This case revolves around the ownership of the daggers. Hopefully, our interviews today will give us some leads we can follow.'

'This is so exciting. Max is jealous, you know. He's the one who had adventures in Hong Kong, and now it's me who's venturing into danger.'

I smothered a snort. I didn't consider interviewing a farmer and the owner of a hardware store to be death defying, but Grace's childish enjoyment of our adventure increased my enthusiasm for the task.

'Quite right. I hope you have your magnifying glass with you.'

She patted her camera bag.

'It's right here, along with my cigarette lighter.'

'What's that for?'

'Plastic melts.'

'Right.'

The Farnhams lived at the end of a rough track full of ruts and potholes. My Mini coped better than I thought it would as I crept along trying to avoid the worst of the dips. We pulled into the farmyard, which had a covering of fresh cow pats, and I parked as close to the back door of the house as I could. The door hung open, and I called out to attract attention. A woman I assumed was Mrs Farnham bustled through the kitchen to greet us.

'You're Tanya Carter, aren't you? I used to love Uncovering the Truth. The whole family would be glued to the screen on a Sunday evening.'

'I'm Tanya Bowe now. This is my colleague, Grace Wong.'

'We'll chat in the sitting room. Would you like a cup of tea?'

'Yes, please,' said Grace.

'Go through and I'll bring in a tray.'

Mr Farnham had come in from the dairy. He still had muck on the legs of his trousers and a piece a straw sticking out of his collar. I resisted the temptation to pluck it out. His wife came in with the tea and tutted.

'Honestly, darling, can you please get tidied up? They want to take a photograph of us.'

'I don't see why I need to smarten up. What you see is what you get.'

She rolled her eyes and sat down to pour us cups of tea. Grace left hers on a newspaper to stop it from marking the table. She took a camera out of Max's bag and struggled to attach a lens.

'I understand that the Farnham family were founder members of the Seacastle coven. It must have been shocking to hear the news about Dot,' I said, hoping to distract them.

'Not as shocking as the method,' said Mrs Farnham. 'I couldn't believe it when I heard that someone had used an athame to do it. That qualifies as blasphemy in my book.'

'Where did you hear that?' I said. 'I didn't know the details had been published yet.'

She blushed crimson and Mr Farnham flashed her a look of annoyance.

'I think it was the Seacastle Herald.'

A lie. I didn't press her on it, but I recorded it in my notebook.

'I found out that Felicity died driving Dot's car. The police think it may have been sabotaged. Can you think of any reason Dot might have been targeted? I understand that relationships amongst the coven members have not always run smoothly.'

Mr Farnham sighed.

'Nobody liked Dot. Her only interest in witchcraft stemmed from her craving for power. She should have been a politician, not a witch. She used her position to frighten people by threatening them with hexes and such like.'

'It was a relief when Felicity came of age and we had a choice. Nobody voted for Dot,' said his wife.

'But who wanted her dead?'

'I doubt very much someone tried to kill her. Frighten her perhaps, but not kill her. Dot used to bet on the horses. She owed money to a local bookie who didn't like to be kept waiting,' said Mr Farnham.

'But she paid him off and got involved with antiques instead of witchcraft. Although I suspect her of magicking up some fakes.'

'Dot didn't suffer from an excess of honesty.'

They both chortled.

'If it's okay with you. I'd like to take a picture of your athame. The police wouldn't let us see the one used to kill Dot,' said Grace.

'Oh no, I don't think so. It's a sacred artefact,' said Mr Farnham.

'I quite understand,' I said. 'But I'd like to see it, if I may, so I can describe it better. I've never seen an athame up close.'

'I don't suppose it will do any harm,' said Mrs Farnham. 'What do you think, dear?'

'I'm in two minds, but okay. I'll get it.'

He left the room and I could hear the staircase creak as he went upstairs.

'Who told you about Dot being murdered with an athame?' I asked Mrs Farnham. 'It's important.'

'Abigail Nash. At the funeral. You were there too, weren't you?'

'Yes. Poor old Abigail. She's been through the wringer, hasn't she?'

'That poor child. Thank goodness for—'

Her husband entered the room holding a package wrapped in a black velvet covering, tied with a piece of silk tasselled cord.

'Thank goodness for what, dear?'

'The rain. I thought the drought would never end.'

I hadn't noticed a recent drought, but I nodded.

Mr Farnham unwrapped the athame with something approaching reverence and laid it on the velvet covering on the table.

'There you are. Inspect it. But no photographs. I've got to go back to the sheds and finish mucking out.'

'Can I get a photograph of you and your wife standing at your front door?' I said.

'Isn't that the photographer's job?'

'Oh, I'm training to take my own photographs. Grace will take one of you in the cowsheds later.'

They shuffled out grumbling and I winked at Grace who handed me one of her cameras. She took the magnifying glass out of her bag and approached the table as we left the room. I took as long as possible taking the photograph, explaining that the light needed to be better and moving them around a lot. By the time I finished, Mr Farnham had become quite grumpy, and he left muttering under his breath. Mrs Farnham led me back indoors, apologising for him.

'All this Dot stuff has unsettled us, you see. These daggers are cursed. We've had nothing but problems with them. Personally, I think Dot was right.'

'About what?'

'She wanted to collect the daggers and sell them. They are worth a fortune. Perpetua thinks they're all contaminated by association with Dot's murder now. We may need to replace them to restore our equilibrium.'

'And what do you think?'

'I think I've already said too much.'

Chapter 25

Grace and I got back into the Mini and I manoeuvred it out of the yard, being careful not to fall into the slurry drain. When we were back on the track leading out to the main road, I turned to her.

'Well?' I said.

'I had a good look at it. I'm sure it's a forgery,' she said. I gasped.

'Oh my goodness. I can't believe it. What on earth's going on?'

'I'm not sure,' she said, shaking her head. 'It's beautifully made, but there's no doubt in my mind. Somebody has replaced the Farnhams' athame with a forged copy.'

'But who could have done it? And when?'

My mind whirred as we drove to the Taylors' house in Lancing. Our discovery seemed to paint a whole new complexion on Dot's murder. If all the daggers had been replaced by someone, maybe Dot had noticed? After all, she had a wide experience with antiques. Could she have been killed to keep her quiet? Or had she herself paid for the forgeries, replaced the originals and been killed because of it?

'You drove past their road,' said Grace.

'Sorry. I lost concentration. We've got half an hour. Do you want a quick sandwich? There's a nice-looking café over there.'

'We might as well.'

In the end, we both had French onion soup with a fresh baguette. The soup tasted as good as it smelled and it revived our spirits for the second interview. Grace explained how to identify a forgery in case I got closer than she did. A tiny cypher on the hasp identified the maker in the originals, but the forger had omitted it. This tiny mark could only be seen using a magnifying glass, but its absence could be spotted with the naked eye. I wondered what we would find at the Taylors' house. Perhaps their dagger had also been stolen or replaced.

I paid the bill, and we drove to their house, a nice semi-detached 1930s building with a garage. The tiny front garden had a manicured front lawn and regimented flower beds. Fiona Taylor opened the newly painted front door and let us into a neat hall with a Persian rug running down its length. A neat row of Wellington boots lined the route to the sitting-room, a cosy room with expensive artwork on the walls and plush armchairs with bright covers. We stood awkwardly at the sitting-room door, waiting to be invited in.

Word had got around about our visit, and everyone wanted their photograph in the newspaper. The sitting-room contained not only the Taylors, David and Fiona, but also three children, and a woman of about ninety who sat scrunched up in a wheelchair with her head bowed onto her chest. I couldn't tell if she was awake or not. After introductions had been made, we all sat around a coffee table which had a package I recognised by its velvet wrapping and silk cord. I nudged Grace, but she didn't react. David Taylor, who looked like Dumbledore from the movies, stroked his long grey beard.

'Come in and sit down over there,' he said, pointing at a sofa with two chocolate labradors sleeping on it. 'Shove the dogs off. They won't mind.'

I took a dim view of those instructions. Grace hung back unwilling to act until one child dragged the dogs off by their collars. David didn't seem to notice.

'I suppose it would be best if I gave you a potted history of the coven and we can work from there?'

'That would be marvellous,' I said, whipping out my notebook.

'Okay then. Sir Nigel Seagrove and his wife Agnes were founder members of the Seacastle coven. Our original coven was composed of twelve witches or six couples. The Seagrove family presented an elaborate dagger to each founding couple to be used as an athame. All the daggers were consecrated in the same ceremony upon the Cissbury Ring.'

'Tell her about the storm, Daddy,' said one little girl with big brown eyes.

'Thunder and lightning rent the skies over Cissbury Ring that night. The auspices were favourable. My mother told me the sky turned red. But they performed the blessing at sunset, so that was hardly surprising really. Nothing like a bit of drama to make the tale more exciting.'

'Were the Parker-Styles family among the founder members of the coven, which first split from the original Brighton coven?'

'Yes, they were.'

'Why was Dot so unpopular with the coven?' I asked, although I already knew.

'She wanted to sell pieces of our heritage to stave off bankruptcy. But other members of the coven were against it. Once she was old enough, they chose Felicity, who had a different father from Dot, a man named Frederick Nash, to be the Parker-Styles family representative. So, Dot got sidelined. But then Felicity died in that awful accident and Dot took over her place in the coven.'

'Felicity had the makings of a great witch. Her aura shone with power and grace. A terrible tragedy to lose her so young,' said Fiona Taylor. 'We were school friends, you know.'

She dabbed the corner of her eye with a tissue.

'May we see the athame?' I asked.

'It's on the table. I will unwrap it for you. Please only hold it using the velvet cloth.'

David Taylor picked up the bundle with reverence and took off the cover. He laid the dagger on the table. Grace handed me the magnifying glass, and I held it up.

'Is it okay if I use this?' I said. 'My eyesight is terrible, and I forgot my glasses.'

'What are you looking for?' said Fiona Taylor.

'The maker's signature,' said the old woman in the wheelchair, lifting her head from her chest. 'Isn't that so, dear?'

Her voice, although weak, vibrated with authority. I didn't risk lying to her.

'That's right. These daggers were made by a famous Chinese artisan. They were stolen from a museum in Hong Kong in the seventeenth century by an ancestor of the Seagroves. They each are worth a fortune, and their combined value is incalculable.'

'They are also of an incalculable value to our coven,' said David Taylor, crossing his arms. 'The longer an athame is used, the more powerful it becomes. We can't recreate that.'

'Do you think that's why Dot was murdered?' said his wife. 'Because of the daggers?'

'Maybe, I don't know yet.'

I had a good look at the dagger and passed it to Grace. After examining it, she shook her head at me. I sighed and turned to the others.

'I'm afraid this dagger is a forgery.'

A gasp echoed around the room. Fiona Taylor sank into her chair with her face in her hands.

'A forgery?' said David Taylor. 'That's impossible. It's been in the family for generations. We've never let it out of our sight.'

'The only person who has seen the dagger except for you is Miles,' said Fiona, lifting her head again.

'Miles? When did you show it to him?'

'I'm not sure. He asked to see it, because… Oh.'

Fiona Taylor put her hand to her mouth. David swore under his breath.

'I don't believe it,' he said.

'I told you there was something odd about his visit,' said the old woman. 'Anyone who is a deviant wants watching if you ask me.'

I ignored her comment.

'Please can somebody explain what happened?' I asked.

'Miles Quirk turned up here one afternoon in a tremendous tizzy. He said he had to see our athame,' said David.

'He told us he had discovered that Dot may have had her dagger copied so she could sell the original. He seemed quite shocked and wanted to see ours so he could compare it with his,' added Fiona.

'I told you he had the mark of the devil on him,' said the old woman, cackling and choking on her own spit. 'But, oh no, who listens to me?'

'Honestly, mother, now is not the time for crowing,' said David. 'Anyway, I gave him ours and he put them both out on the velvet cloth to compare them. After a while, he sighed with relief and said he was mistaken. He apologised for having worried us.'

'Then he wrapped up his athame and left,' said Fiona. 'Only he must have switched them when we weren't looking. I can't believe I fell for it. A cheap circus trick like that.'

She shook her head in disgust.

'I wonder how many times he's carried out the same deception,' said Grace. 'I didn't tell the Farnhams, but their athame is fake too.'

'That's appalling,' said Fiona. 'Do they know?'

'Not yet,' said Grace.

'I'm sorry,' I said, standing up. 'We need to confirm what happened with them right away.'

'You'll get it back for us, won't you?' said David. 'It's part of our heritage.'

'I'll do my best,' I said. 'But it's more complicated than that.'

'It's part of my heritage too,' said Grace. 'I'm from Hong Kong.'

Silence greeted this statement. I don't suppose they had ever wondered about the origin of the daggers before, or whether they had any right to them. I tugged Grace's arm, and we stood up to leave. Fiona saw us out, still tearful, and we headed for the car.

After we left the Taylors' house, I drove a short way before parking on the side of the road. I called the Farnhams' number and Mrs Farnham picked up the phone.

'Hello?'

'Yes, hello, Mrs Farnham, It's Tanya Bowe again.'

'What do you want? My husband didn't like you at all. He thinks you were up to something fishy, like in one of your investigations.'

'I'm sorry you're upset. I need to ask you an important question about Miles Quirk. Have you seen him lately?'

'We have, not that it's any of your business.'

'Did he come to your house to look at your athame?'

'What's going on?'

Mr Farnham had taken the phone from his wife, and his voice shuddered with anger.

'This is important. I need to know if Miles Quirk came to your house and asked to see your athame recently.'

'He did, as it happens. He said he had reason to believe it might be a fake. I gave it to him so he could compare it with his. He's been a member of the coven since his mother died, you know.'

'Has he? What did he say about the athame?'

'He said they were identical and he must have been mistaken. He gave it back to me and he left.' He cleared his throat. 'We believed him of course. After all, he's an expert. But now I want to ask you a question. Was the real reason for your visit a check on the authenticity of the dagger?'

'I'm afraid so. We think somebody may have made copies of one dagger and have swapped them out with the real ones.'

I heard a sharp intake of breath.

'And ours?'

'My colleague examined it and I'm sorry to tell you, but it's a forgery.'

'And you think Miles may have taken the real one?'

'I don't know yet.'

'He'll regret it if he has. You can't fool around with magic. Will we get it back?'

'I'm not sure. Please let the police deal with it. I promise to keep you informed.'

Chapter 26

I dropped a stunned Grace back at her front door and drove home. My mind raced with possibilities. I needed to talk to Mouse and run through the case with him. I hoped he had not made other arrangements. I needed to talk to him about his future, but I didn't know how to approach the subject or what to suggest. My father would have recommended a few years in the army to straighten him out. I know what Harry would have said. Both he and Nick were damaged goods after their stints in the Middle East and Northern Ireland. Mouse did not strike me as someone who would thrive in those environments. His reaction to losing his phantom sibling told me all I needed to know about his soft core.

I parked the car and ran through the rain to the Grotty Hovel. Unbeknownst to me, my left boot had sprung a leak and my sock absorbed half a puddle. I squelched my way indoors. The sitting room felt cold and empty. Hades popped his head above the parapets of his laundry basket and then lowered it again. I could almost feel his disappointment. His list of favourite humans did not include me, although he found it easy to convince me he had not been fed if he put his mind to it. I went into the kitchen and opened the fridge door. A quick glance reminded me I should have gone to the supermarket on my way home. I shut it. Then I opened it again in desperation. Food had not appeared since my last visit. I wondered if an athame might help magic some up.

I felt exhausted and depressed. My stomach rumbled in protest at the time it had been empty. I shouted up the stairs, but there was no answer. Mouse had gone out again. My worries about him increased as I fretted about the company he was keeping. Tears of frustration leaked from my eyes and I sank onto the sofa with a tissue. My cell phone rang, and I pulled it out of my handbag, hoping it would be Harry. I needed his reassurance so badly, but I felt bad leaning on him when I knew his problems were also weighing him down. To my intense disappointment, DI Antrim's number had come up on the screen. I considered ignoring the call, but my curiosity overcame my reluctance.

'Hello,' I said, meaning to sound normal, but to my embarrassment, my voice caught in my throat.

'It's Terry, DI Antrim. Are you okay?'

'Not really. I'm starving and there's nothing in the fridge and Mouse is missing and the case is a disaster.'

I sniffed loudly.

'Hm. This sounds serious. Would you like a takeaway and we can discuss the case together? If you would be comfortable with that? Otherwise, I can drop the food in and go home.'

'Actually, that sounds wonderful. Can I have fish and chips, please?'

'I'll put the blue light on and be right with you.'

I know what you're thinking, but, honestly, if Godzilla had offered me food, I'd have invited him in. I needed to discuss the developments of the day with somebody familiar with the cases, and I could only imagine how cross Helen would have been if I had borrowed George again. Since they had got together, I had realised how much I still relied on our cosy chats about ongoing cases. We had found middle ground since our divorce and

Sharon's demise. We weren't friends exactly, but we had mutual respect going. I fancied a glass of wine, but DI Antrim could not drink and drive, so I made a pot of tea and waited for him to arrive.

Half an hour later, we were sitting at the table shovelling portions of chips onto our plates and breaking the crispy batter of the pieces of cod with eager knifes. The first mouthful tasted like manna to me. I shut my eyes in bliss, and when I opened them, he was trying not to laugh at me.

'I'm hungry,' I said. 'I've had a tough day.'

'What do you want to talk about first?' he asked.

'Forged daggers. I visited two of the other families who belong to the Seacastle coven, and both of their daggers had been replaced with fakes. Miles Quirk paid them a visit, claiming to be checking on their authenticity, but he may have switched the real ones out and replaced them with fakes.'

'Or he may really have been checking. I seem to remember he suspected Dot of replacing artefacts with fakes so she could sell them.'

'But what if he misdirected the investigation to Dot to take any suspicion away from him? She's dead, so you can't ask her anymore.'

'That's true,' I admitted. 'But when did she take their daggers? I'm sure they wouldn't let Dot near them after they found out she intended to sell some of the coven's heritage,' said DI Antrim, helping himself to another piece of cod.

'He is the only member of the coven with sufficient expertise to recognise the value of the daggers. Dot knew the price of everything, but the value of nothing. She just ran the fair to squeeze as much cash as she could out of the stallholders. And he had a motive. He believed Dot had sabotaged the car driven by Felicity.'

'Haven't you told him about it being Dot's car yet?'

'No. I haven't seen him since Grace and I talked to him in her shop. He admitted to hating Dot, but he told me she wouldn't have killed Felicity.'

'I still think it would be worth talking to him again. Maybe we could organise a little chat at the station? I'll ask George if he wants to be there with us.'

'You want me to be there?'

'I think it would be useful. After all, you interviewed the families. Now, what's all this about young Mouse?'

The fact he referred to Mouse by his nickname and didn't call him Andy like George insisted on doing, made me relax. I needed to talk to someone neutral who wouldn't accuse me of fussing over the boy, and the calm way he munched his supper made me confident he did not intend to judge. So, I told him about Mouse's background and his dodgy friends and the hacking and how much I loved him despite it all, and ended up crying again.

'I know he's not my son,' I said. 'But he belongs with me, and I'm the only one who really cares about him. Except George, but he's worse than useless. And I want to give him good advice, but I don't know what a teenage hacker could do as a career, or if he'd even accept suggestions from me.'

I paused for breath, embarrassed, and ate a chip to play for time.

'I had a boy who would be his age now,' DI Antrim said, so softly that I almost missed it. 'I loved him more than life itself. But he found drugs, or they found him.'

I thought my heart would stop beating as I watched him swallow and fight back his emotions. The universe slowed down as I waited for him to tell me what I knew in that awful instant.

'I lost him five years ago.' He gulped. 'I know all about worry, and boys who stay out too late and hang out with unsuitable friends. Far more than you can imagine.'

I didn't move. It felt like time had stopped altogether as I fought for the right thing to say. What on earth could that be? At that moment, Hades emerged from his basket and leapt onto the table via the sofa, mistiming his jump and sending chips flying everywhere. I grabbed him and couldn't help laughing.

'Have I introduced you to my other stepson?' I asked. 'No dodgy friends. Only dodgy manners.'

We cleaned up the table and sat back down.

'I'm so sorry,' I said. 'I didn't know. George—'

'Oh, George doesn't know. He's not one for chit chat.'

'That's true.'

'Look, I only told you because I want you to trust my motives. I think I have a solution for Mouse, but you'll have to leave it with me. Is that okay?'

'Yes. Of course. I'd be so grateful.'

'It would be my pleasure, but I have a favour to ask in return.'

'Anything within reason,' I said, smiling.

'Could you please call me Terry? DI Antrim sounds like he's got a stick up his arse.'

When Terry, yes, I'm going to call him that now, left, I had a glass of wine and wrote notes on the case. Mouse turned up around midnight and beamed when he saw me still awake. He came over and put his arms around my shoulders and snuggled in to my neck. He sniffed my hair, making me laugh.

'How much have you had to drink?'

'Enough, I think. Lots maybe.'

'Hm. You smell like a brewery. Did you have a good time?'

'Sort of. It's quite boring talking about football for hours.'

I couldn't help smiling. Mouse liked to hang out with middle-aged women far more than with lads his own age. He loved the attention and the hugs, especially fragrant hugs like those given by Ghita and Flo. He would sit back and listen to Roz gossiping about the residents of Seacastle for hours without complaint. He liked to make people's favourite coffee and put hearts into the foam. I had to trust him not to get involved in the darker side of Seacastle's social scene. The smell of weed on the promenade could not be ignored on a sunny day, when people lit up on the beach. I hadn't smelled cigarettes on his clothes, so I hope that was a good sign.

'Do you want a glass of wine?'

'I don't think so. I'll just make myself a tea. Do you want one?'

'Yes, please. There have been big developments in the case today. Do you want to hear about them?'

'I do, but you'll have to tell me again tomorrow. I think I'll go to bed now instead of making tea. Is that okay?'

'Of course, sweetheart. It's lovely to have you at home. The Grotty Hovel is cold and lonely without you.'

'You need to make Harry move in. Why don't you get married?'

'We will. He's lost his van though, so I don't think it's number one on his list right now.'

'What happened?'

'The engine blew.'

'And I haven't talked to him about it. I feel terrible. Too much drinking.'

'You can call him in the morning. Why don't you go with him on a clearance? He'd like that.'

Mouse grinned.

'I would too. Night-night.'

He went up the stairs, patting his pockets, and I knew he would text Harry right away. My two boys. My heart felt full. I hoped Terry would find something worthy of Mouse, so I could sleep soundly again.

Chapter 27

The next morning, I woke to find the sun shining in a blue sky with small fluffy clouds. My heart lightened, and I sang in the shower with a gusto I hadn't managed for ages. Harry had bought me a waterproof radio so I could sing along to classic hits any time I fancied. When I opened the package, I knew he was the only man for me, and I'm even more sure now. I wondered how on earth we were going to buy another van, even with our combined finances. There had to be a way. I got dressed and made myself a tea in my travel cup for taking to the wind shelter. I had been neglecting to feed Herbert the herring gull, and I didn't want him to think I had abandoned him for good.

Chilly air greeted me as I shut the front door and I stood on the doorstep debating the wisdom of my choice of coat. I went back inside to put on something warmer and wrap a scarf around my neck. I hate to be cold, and as the Swedes say, 'there is no bad weather, only bad clothes'. I stepped outside and then swore as I had to go back inside yet again to rescue Herbert's scraps from my other coat pocket. I set out for the wind shelter being buffeted by the westerly blowing along the coast. When I reached it, I saw that somebody else had already had the same idea. From the silhouette, I knew Helen had got there first. She looked up as I came around the corner and attempted a smile.

'Hello stranger,' she said. 'How's the case proceeding? George is all agog with the goings on in the coven. I don't think he had witches on his Bingo card for this murder inquiry.'

'Who did? I didn't even know they were still a thing. I thought they had been consigned to history and movies.'

'His mood's taken a hit. He struggles when he's not in control.'

I heard the unspoken complaint and patted her hand.

'He's rather old-fashioned, but you should know that by now.'

'What did you used to do when he turned grumpy?'

'Cooking his favourite food and telling him he was wonderful always worked.'

'I'm sorry I took his side in your divorce. The more I see of him, the more I realise how unsuited you were.'

'Don't be sorry. Nobody knows what marriages are like from the outside. I thought you and Martin were blissfully happy.'

'So did I. For a long time. I feel so much safer with George. He'd never hurt me.'

'Don't let him be grumpy with you. Remind him not to bring his work home with him.'

'Are we past the honeymoon stage already? We're not even married yet.'

'Do you want to be?'

'I doubt George would try marriage again. At this rate, he'll have to change his name to Henry.'

Herbert arrived with a kerfuffle of wings and beak, making us both jump. I reached into my pocket and pulled out his bag of snacks and threw them for him one by one.

'You spoil that bird,' said Helen. 'You spoil everyone. Mouse is living the life of Larry at your house.'

'He needs love. That's not the same as spoiling him. Anyway, Terry is looking into something for Mouse to do.'

Helen guffawed.

'Terry? Since when is DI Antrim Terry? Is there something I should know?'

I blushed despite myself.

'He asked me to call him that. We have been working together on this case, because Dot Parker-Styles's sister died in a suspicious accident twenty years ago and he attended the site as a young PC.'

'What a coincidence! What does Harry think of you and DI Antrim getting all friendly?'

'We are not getting all friendly!'

'Whoa there. I was only joking. He seems like a nice man.'

'He lost his son,' I said. 'To drugs. That's why he wants to help Mouse.'

Helen's face fell.

'Oh no. How dreadful. I'm sorry.'

'Me too. I almost cried when he told me. I'm pretty sure he doesn't fancy me. He just doesn't have any friends.'

'Coppers are useless at the soft stuff.'

'George will get better if you force him. Sharon was making good headway before…'

'I know. I will try. He's lovely to me most of the time. Are you finding it weird we are together?'

'It seems like the most natural thing in the world.'

Helen hugged me and I leaned in. George had brought us together again and for that I would always love him.

I left soon afterward for Second Home, striding down the promenade to stay ahead of the bank of drizzle which approached Seacastle. When I turned into the High Street, I took a detour to look into the window of Surfusion and admired the décor. I looked up at the small statue of Ganesha which sat in the glass alcove above the door, bringing good fortune to all who entered. If anticipation equalled success, they were milking it for all it was worth. I couldn't wait for them to inaugurate the place. Ghita had told me the opening should be imminent, but so far, no date had been fixed.

The smell of coffee and furniture polish hit me as I entered Second Home. Out of habit, I ran my fingers over a table to check for dust and found none. I needed a big clearance to keep myself occupied. It occurred to me that Max and Grace owed me a favour. I wondered if Max would lend Harry his van if we got a clearance. I took my phone out of my bag to call them, but I had a message from George to meet him at the station with DI Antrim at eleven, as they had called Miles Quirk in for a chat. He suggested bringing Grace. I wondered how Miles would react to being interviewed by a panel. He had been quite defensive with me and Grace. What effect would the two DIs have on him?

I rang Grace and asked her if she would like to come to the station with me. She squeaked with excitement, which I took as a yes. Then I asked her about the van. Silence followed. I waited her out.

'If Harry borrows the van, can I use him to help me too?'

'I'll have to check, but I don't see why not. He's done it before.'

In fact, I used to have reservations about Harry working with Grace, but she never tried to poach him. It would have been peculiar now we were a couple. Even Grace would not go that far for commerce. Hopefully. I made myself a coffee and ate a piece of lemon and lime drizzle. The breakfast of champions.

Feeling reinforced with the cake sticking to my ribs, I set off down the High Street to pick up Grace. The drizzle had become heavier, and the streets shone wet under my feet. People had retreated indoors or were huddled under umbrellas. The Asian Emporium's window drew me in as usual with its coordinated selection of eclectic treasure. Grace spotted me gazing in and waved. She came straight out, opening her umbrella, which had a cloud of bright orange butterflies on it. Her lemon-yellow raincoat almost reached the ground where it met her scarlet boots. It made me smile. She had dressed for battle.

'Let's go,' she said. 'We can't be late.'

Chapter 28

The station loomed through the gloom, offering us shelter from the rain, which had become heavier, forming deep puddles on the streets. We had to skirt around them to avoid being soaked by passing cars. We dashed up the steps and into reception. Sally Wright tutted as we dripped water all over her floor.

'Somebody will go flying on that wet patch. I'll have to get the cleaner in,' she said, her blonde curls bouncing with indignation.

'I believe DI Carter is expecting us,' I said, ignoring her fake umbrage.

'And DI Antrim,' said Terry, sweeping into the station in his poncho, like a black crow, and bringing more water inside. 'Follow me, ladies.'

He pressed the code into the pad on the door and swung it open. Grace and I passed into the inner sanctum of the station as Sally emerged with a mop to dry the floor. She gave us a glare, but I just smiled back at her. She could be moody, but she could also be sweet and kind when she felt like it. As usual, the heating had been set at tropical and the pungent smell of feet made us wrinkle our noses at each other in disgust. DI Antrim shooed us into the interview room where it was cooler and smelled of air freshener. George sat at the table with a stack of papers by his left elbow. I knew he used them to intimidate suspects by pretending to consult them during interviews, as if he had piles of evidence already.

We sat on the uncomfortable metal chairs under the blinking fluorescent lights. The walls were bare except for a torn poster advising people of their right to have a solicitor present. I restrained myself from biting my nails, but I could feel my shoulders tighten with expectation. PC Brennan popped in with a tray containing a stainless-steel teapot and five mugs. Terry pulled the tray towards him.

'I'll be mother,' he said.

He poured us all a cup, but Grace refused hers. She didn't like strong 'builders' tea, only jasmine and pekoe teas without milk or sugar. She accepted a glass of water, but she took only one sip before abandoning it. Our anticipation rose while we waited for Miles to turn up. My stomach churned, making me feel sick. Could Miles be the murderer? It didn't seem possible, but he had passionate beliefs, and that can be reason enough sometimes. I took out my notebook and reviewed my notes about our meetings so far and reminded myself of the contradictions in his behaviour. Grace sat in a Zen-like silence; her hands folded in her lap. At one stage, she put her head on one side as if considering something.

George shuffled his papers and looked around in annoyance.

'Where is he? Shouldn't he be here by now?'

The door opened on cue, and PC Brennan showed Miles Quirk into the room. He had dialled down his flamboyant style for the interview and had on a brown corduroy suit and a black polo neck. On seeing all of us, he looked around and wavered at the door.

'Please sit down,' said Terry.

Miles pulled out a chair on our side of the table and sat sideways, as if he might flee at any moment. A bead of sweat appeared on his forehead.

'For your information,' said George. 'You are not under arrest. This is a voluntary process. You may leave at any time. You may also request a solicitor if you require one. We have asked you here today because Ms Bowe and Mrs Wong have been researching a set of antique daggers for us and your name came up during their investigations. Do you wish to proceed?'

'I can go?' said Miles.

'I don't recommend it,' said Terry. 'If we have to interview you under caution, things will be a lot less relaxed. Can I pour you a cup of tea?'

Miles glanced at me, and I gave him what I hoped was a reassuring smile. He nodded.

'Yes, please. No sugar and just a dash of milk.'

'Great,' said George. 'We'll start at the beginning if that's okay with you?'

Miles nodded again, sipping his tea and glancing over the brim at us.

'Over to you, DI Antrim,' said George.

'I understand you are a member of the Seacastle coven, a hereditary position. Is that correct?'

'Yes, I am.'

'And through this membership, you became acquainted with Dorothy Parker-Styles and Felicity Nash who were sisters and lived in the same house?'

'Yes. I've known them since I can remember. Well, knew them anyway. And the other families in the coven. We were all friends as children. It was only natural...'

He petered off and chewed at one of his nails.

'I'm sorry for your loss. Dot's death must have come as a great shock to you, especially after already losing Felicity, of whom I believe you were very fond.'

'It was horrendous. Like a nightmare. I've been distressed ever since.'

'Did you like Dorothy Parker-Styles?' said George.

Miles barked out a laugh.

'Who did? She was the most unpleasant and dishonest person in Seacastle.'

'Let's get back to the death of Felicity, if that's alright, DI Carter?' said Terry.

George grunted his assent.

'We have re-investigated the car accident which killed Felicity Nash, and some fresh evidence has come to light.'

'Did you find out who killed her?' said Miles, suddenly animated.

'Not exactly. But I think we have established that Felicity was not the intended victim of the accident. She drove off in Dot's car, which crashed because someone had interfered with the brakes.'

The blood drained from Miles' face.

'Flic died by mistake?'

His head dropped into his hands. Nobody spoke. He raised it again. His eyes were red with grief.

'But who would kill Dot? I know she had enemies everywhere, but I can't imagine anyone bothering to kill her. She had no power and had to behave herself because of her run in with the law.'

'How about Roy Loveday?' asked Terry.

'Roy? He couldn't have done it.'

'Why do you say that?' said George.

'Because Dot wouldn't allow him anywhere near the house. He was in Lewes the day of the crash, on a job.'

'How do you know that?'

'Because I rang his house and talked to his mother. Have you spoken to him? He'll tell you.'

'And how do you know about Roy and Felicity?' said Terry.

'Flic told me everything, always. We were best friends.' Miles ran his fingers through his hair. He shook his head in disbelief. 'You're telling me that somebody sabotaged Dot's car and killed Flic by mistake? They must have lived with that knowledge all these years. But why didn't they try again?'

'Maybe protecting Abigail? Dot wasn't much of a mother, but she was better than nothing,' I interjected.

'Let's get back to the present day,' said George. 'Where were you when Dot was murdered?'

'At home with my partner. He can vouch for me.'

'Did you know someone stabbed her with an athame?'

Miles gasped and froze with shock.

'I don't believe it,' he croaked. 'This can't be happening.'

'Did you know the athame used was a copy of the original?'

Miles grabbed on to the edge of the table to steady himself. I thought he might faint for a moment.

'Another forgery? I don't believe it. How…'

He looked up to find us all staring at him.

'How long have you known about the forgeries?' said George. 'This is important. Please answer truthfully.'

Miles took a swig of his tea and rocked back and forwards in his chair, blinking. Finally, he put down his cup and spoke.

'Um, well, I don't know when the switch was made, but I noticed my athame had been stolen and replaced last year. I took it out for a Wicca ritual I wanted to perform, and it felt different in my hand. The dagger looked identical, but the weight seemed different somehow. More blade heavy. I examined it with a magnifying glass and I noticed it lacked the maker's mark. It shocked me profoundly. It was as if someone had stolen one of my organs without me noticing.'

'What were your first instincts about what had happened to it?' asked George.

'I have to admit, the first person I thought of was Dot. I even went to see her. But she laughed in my face and told me not to invent stories.'

'Did you believe her?'

'I did. She seemed bemused I would accuse her of such a thing. She showed me her dagger. It had not been switched.'

'Is that when you went to see the Farnhams?' I asked.

He blinked twice.

'So much for secrets,' he said. 'Yes, I checked their dagger and the one belonging to the Taylors. They were both fakes. I couldn't believe it.'

'Why didn't you tell them their daggers were forgeries?'

'I'm not sure. I felt responsible somehow.'

'And you weren't?' said George.

'I'm not sure how to explain this to outsiders, but being a member of the coven is a sacred duty. Dot was like a rotten apple contaminating the barrel. I felt if I told the others about the daggers, maybe our bonds would be irreversibly broken. I hoped to find the source of the forgeries and force them to replace the real ones without anyone noticing. Naïve of me, I know.'

'So, you don't know who replaced the daggers?'

'None. I swear.'

He dropped his head. His bewilderment was palpable. I felt enormous sympathy for him as his world crumbled around him.

'Do you have any idea who could have made such perfect replicas?'

His head came up again.

'Oh, yes. That I can tell you. His name is Cyril Wender. He goes by the name of Jasper Christie. If anyone can tell you who replaced the daggers, it's him. In fact, he's the only person who knows, besides the murderer.'

'Why haven't you asked him about who ordered the daggers?'

'Because he's unpredictable, and I worried he would target me. I had hoped to find out by a process of elimination.'

'Do you know where we can find him?'

Miles smiled for the first time.

'That I can help you with.'

After Miles Quirk left, George sent us home too.

'I need to organise a raid on this fellow's house, and you can't be involved.'

'George is right,' said Terry. 'This Wender person may be dangerous. He's realised his dagger was used to kill by now. He may even have killed Dot himself. I expect he's on edge.'

I couldn't keep the disappointment off my face. This would be the climax of the investigation and we were being excluded. George patted my hand.

'I promise to keep you informed of the results, but this should give us the last clue to piece this mystery together. You've both been great, but we need to call it a day on your consultancy for now. Please go home.'

Grace stood up to go, but then she wavered.

'What's up, Mrs Wong?' said Terry.

'Am I still a suspect?' she asked.

Chapter 29

I couldn't have been more disappointed about our dismissal from the case, despite being well aware that our cooperation with the police was bound to end sooner or later. Grace did not seem to mind. She couldn't wait to go home and tell Max about her adventure. She found it much easier than I did to accept authority. I had a rebellious streak, which didn't diminish with time. Mouse and Harry tried to cheer me up when I got home, but I resisted their attempts. I took to my bed and pulled the duvet over my head. Even Hades putting his head around the door to see what the kerfuffle was about didn't make me feel better.

The next morning, I sulked through breakfast, toying with my cereals and sighing theatrically. I was still in my pyjamas and intended on heading straight back to bed for another bout of self-pity. Finally, even Harry, the most patient man on the planet, got irritated with me.

'For heaven's sake, buck up,' he said. 'Stop behaving like somebody took your toy at the kindergarten.'

'They did. I wanted to see the arrest. They wouldn't have got anywhere without me.'

'And Grace.'

'Her too.'

'Did you ask her about the van?'

I sniffed.

'I did.'

'And?'

'She'll lend it to you on condition you help her move stuff like you did last time.'

'Really? Well, that's the best news I've heard all day. Get dressed and stop behaving like a toddler.'

'I don't want to. I thought I'd stay in bed all day and moulder.'

'I'm sure Grace will come with me if you won't.'

Despite myself, I felt my excitement rising.

'We've got a clearance?'

'An excellent one. Ring Grace and ask her for the van. If she will let us have it, I'll inform the woman that we'll be there today.'

To my surprise, Grace's voice sounded as if she had not got out of bed yet. She agreed to lend us the van without a quibble. From the way she was whispering, I suspected they had over-celebrated her definitive removal from the suspects list. I wished her a nice day and said we'd collect the keys. I gave Harry the thumbs up and he poured himself another cup of tea.

'Get dressed,' he said. 'Or I'll go without you.'

Soon we were on the road under blue skies with bands of thick white cloud hanging low over the channel. The wind farm stood out against the sky like a field of dragonflies balanced on blades of grass. A smell of freshly cut grass blew through the cabin. We turned off the coast road and headed north up a series of progressively narrower lanes into the green oasis of the South Downs. Trees hung with blossom released clouds of petals onto the roads as the gentle breeze blew through their branches. I felt as if we were entering an enchanted realm, and my bad mood lifted and floated away with the petals. Harry beamed as he noticed the change.

'This is going to be a great one. I feel it in my bones,' he said.

'Fingers crossed.'

We arrived at a quaint cottage with a thatched roof, surrounded by a picket fence on its last legs, its paint peeling and several posts rotten through. More trees full of apple blossom framed the cottage and gave it a fairy tale air. I half expected Snow White to step out to greet us. I couldn't have been more wrong. It was the wicked stepsister with a cigarette dangling from her lips.

'What time do you call this?' she said, looking at her watch. 'You're late.'

'I don't think so,' said Harry. 'I told you we'd be coming only forty-five minutes ago, and the teleporter is out of order.'

'Well, I've got a timetable, even if you haven't. I need the place cleared today.'

'We'll get right on it,' said Harry. 'I presume you have removed any items of sentimental value from the property?'

'There weren't nothing I wanted from my mother-in-law in life, snobby cow. And I don't need any mementos of her, now she's gone. Take it all and shut the door after you.'

'Right you are, then. We'll get on, shall we?'

She flicked her cigarette into the roses and stalked off. Seconds later, her car left, heading for the coast at well over the speed limit.

'Nice woman,' I said. 'If you like that sort of thing.'

Harry laughed.

'Ghastly old bat. Come on. Let's see if we have better luck today.'

The cottage had a Dutch door, and I imagined leaving the top half open on a sunny day to let the light stream indoors. Harry pushed through it into a bright sitting room and stood there in amazement. Not only did the room appear untouched, but a cup and saucer still sat on a side table beside an armchair facing a television set. An imprint of the last person to sit in the chair could still be made out. I stared at it, stunned, unable to remove the idea from my mind that the owner of the cottage had died in that chair.

'That's a turn up for the books,' said Harry. 'I know they used to make death masks of people when they died, but nobody mentioned body casts.'

'This place hasn't been touched. They picked her up, took her away and shut the door.'

'I know it's upsetting, but she's dead, so she won't mind. Let's give her belongings a new life. It's lucky Grace's van is bigger than mine. This is going to be a tight squeeze.'

The cottage had four rooms; a kitchen and a sitting room on the ground floor and two bedrooms upstairs. We started upstairs, using plastic bags we found in the kitchen, and emptied her wardrobes and chests of drawers of linen, clothes, shoes and sundries. I noticed the jewellery boxes were empty; they had time to loot her bedroom at least. It made me incandescent with rage, but I had seen her daughter-in-law's attitude, so I knew what meant something to her and what didn't. I found some nice beaded handbags from the 1920s that I knew Grace could sell, so I kept them separate. Once the metal beds were stripped, Harry dismantled them and I helped him to stagger downstairs with the pieces. They would sell well in London, so I let Harry take them. The wardrobes and chest of drawers were not valuable either.

It didn't take us as long as I had expected to clear the upstairs. Since nobody had touched the kitchen, we could make ourselves a cup of tea with powdered milk to wash down some Shortcake biscuits. The owner of the cottage still had kitchen bowls and storage jars from the sixties and seventies in her cupboards, so I put those in boxes for Second Home. The kitchen furniture was classic early Conran, which made me rub my hands together in glee. Harry did not comment much. He concentrated on removing items from the cottage and packing the van.

When I got to the last room, I found myself spooked by the chair and its ghostly occupant. The brooding silence of the sitting room brought me down to earth with a bump. Was it a bad omen? I turned to Harry, who also seemed reluctant to touch it.

'Can we leave this here?' I said. 'I know it sounds odd, but I don't want to move it. It feels as if it's cursed.'

Harry smiled.

'Not odd at all. Why don't you leave the side table and the cup and saucer as well? Just in case.'

I gave him a hug. We emptied the contents of her art deco glass walled cabinet into another box. Twee Wade ornaments of no value formed the bulk of the contents. The owner must have liked owls, because an entire shelf was monopolised by their squat figures with enormous eyes. Two nice fifties armchairs and some other period furniture rounded off my haul for the day.

We worked until dark, loading the van, and we were ready to go. The house sat empty except for the chair and side table with its empty cup. A chill crept in through the door and enveloped the entire house. I shivered.

'Let's get out of here.'

We shut the door and got into the van.

'Have you got everything?' said Harry.

'I think so. Wait, where's my phone?'

'Your phone? I don't remember seeing it.'

'I haven't checked it all day. We've been so busy.'

After a quick search, I discovered it in the side pocket of the van's passenger door. I didn't remember placing it there. Perhaps it fell while I was getting out. I checked the screen and found a dozen or more messages from George waiting for me.

'Blast it. I missed zillions of messages from George. I guess he's crowing over the arrest.'

'Open them.'

I tapped on the first one and the phone fell out of my hand into Harry's footwell. I rolled my eyes and turned to Harry in supplication. He rescued the phone, grunting with effort, and read the message I had opened. His eyes widened, and he handed it back to me.

'I don't believe it,' he said. 'Cyril Wender has been found dead. You'd better ring George right away.'

'Dead, but how? This is a nightmare.'

My mind filled with dozens of scenarios. Had the murderer struck again? Maybe Wender's death was unrelated to the daggers. He had an unsavoury reputation.

George picked up his phone on the first ring.

'Where have you been? I've been calling you for hours.'

'Sorry. We're on a job. I left my phone in the van.'

'Can I drop in tonight and tell you about Wender?'

'Sure. We'll be home in about forty-five minutes if the traffic isn't bad. Budget for an hour and bring a takeaway for four or five if Helen's coming?'

'Anything else, your majesty?'

'I'd like a lamb korma and some poppadums please. What about you, Harry?'

Chapter 30

We drove home without emptying the van, as Grace did not need us to return it for a couple of days. All my joy at the beautiful countryside had faded as I willed us to hurry home faster. I couldn't believe what had happened. Had the murderer struck again to cover their tracks? I took out my notebook and read and reread my notes about the case. Nothing stood out to me about Wender. His alter-ego Christie had been rude and abrasive, and he appeared to benefit from his supposed association with Dot. Had someone killed him to stop him from being revealed as the forger of the daggers?

The only comment I couldn't square with the others I had noted down was from Veronica Higgins who had claimed Wender had left a dagger for sale on her stall. She had described it as having a black wooden blade with snakes on the hilt. She had also suggested Roy Loveday had stolen it while she had gone for coffee. With what I knew now, I suspected the dagger of being a fake. But why leave it on the Higgins' table? Did he expect to use it later? I sighed.

'Hang in there,' said Harry. 'Your blood sugar must be on the floor. We'll be home soon. Have you got a jelly baby or a toffee in your bag?'

How well he knew me already. I rooted around and found a couple of jelly babies lurking in the side pocket with my lipsticks. The shot of sugar went straight into my veins and I felt calmer.

'This is when I regret giving up smoking,' I said.

'Can you imagine Grace's reaction if you smoked in her van? She'd find a dagger to stick in you too.'

I snorted with laughter at the mental picture.

'True. She's a little possessive about her van, but I think she was hungover this morning. She didn't put up any resistance when I asked to borrow it.'

'I can't believe they don't have any way of playing music in here.'

'Would you like me to sing?'

'I will not answer that on the grounds you might hit me and make me crash.'

We parked outside the house and went inside. Mouse beamed when he saw Harry and gave him a big hug. His face fell as he read my expression.

'Another bad clearance? I'm sorry,' he said, hugging me too.

'No, on the contrary, we've got a van full of goodies,' said Harry.

'What happened then?' said Mouse. 'Tanya didn't turn you down again, did she?'

He laughed. 'I've given up asking for now.'

'Leave Harry alone. I'm allowed to take my time. Anyway, it's nothing to do with him. I—'

The doorbell rang and Mouse ran to answer it. George stood at the door with a large bag of takeaway from our local Indian restaurant. He put out his hand for Mouse to shake, but Mouse ignored it and hugged George too. I smothered a smile as I watched George pretend not to enjoy it.

'Knives and forks,' I said. 'I'll get the plates.'

Harry helped me get the table set, and he opened a bottle of wine. We all sat down, opened the boxes and served ourselves. Nobody spoke in the beginning. We were like a pack of ravenous wolves with our snouts in a hot carcass. The spicy curry invaded my taste buds and nasal passages, making my eyes water. I stole forkfuls from everybody else's plates until I could eat no longer. Mouse also rubbed his tummy and declared himself full to the agreement of the others who groaned and patted theirs too. I sent him to the kitchen to put on the kettle while we cleared the table of empty boxes and dirty cutlery.

'How did your clearance go today?' asked George. 'I saw Grace's van outside.'

'Pretty good, until I got your message,' I said.

George sighed and fidgeted with a pen, clicking the end, until I removed it from his grasp.

'It's not the news I was expecting either, but at least we have the murderer.'

'What do you mean?'

Mouse shouted from the kitchen. 'Don't tell them yet. I can't hear.'

We all moved to the couch and armchairs. I kept my glass of wine with me, hoping it would numb the pain of the revelation about Jasper/Cyril. Mouse served tea to George and Harry and then sat beside me on the sofa. Hades sat on his lap and hissed at me when I tried to stroke him. Maggot!

'Go on, Dad,' said Mouse. 'We're all agog.'

George sat up straighter in the armchair.

'This morning, I set out in my car with DI Antrim to Cyril Wender's house, with two squad cars acting as back up. We didn't know if there would be any trouble, but we didn't take any chances. The house was nothing exceptional. It's a semi-detached modern building in a cul-de-sac. I sent some lads around to the back of the house to prevent Wender from fleeing the scene, and then we knocked on the door. We tried for five minutes, but couldn't get an answer, so we left PC Brennan on the front door and went around the back. A large shed sat at the end of the garden, and I noticed the door hung open, so DI Antrim and I went to check it. We couldn't open it fully because Wender lay on the floor inside with a dagger in his stomach.'

'Like Dot?' I said.

'Just like that,' said George. 'His blood had pooled around him, so we're pretty sure he died right there. Anyway, we climbed into forensic jumpsuits to avoid contaminating the scene and had a quick look around the shed. It had been used as a work shop for creating forgeries so it was full of tools and paints and so on. Anyway, upon looking around, I noticed a letter on the work bench addressed to me.'

'You? How creepy,' said Mouse, admiration in his voice.

'It was a bit,' said George, pleased.

'What did it say?' said Harry.

'Wender had written it before he died. In it, he confessed to the murder of Dot Parker-Styles and claimed she had forced him to make a forged set of daggers for her. He had got greedy and made extra daggers and she had confronted him about it. That's when he stabbed her. He claimed it was in the heat of the moment, but now he couldn't live with what he'd done.'

'He stabbed himself with a dagger?' I said. 'Wouldn't that be difficult?'

'Verging on the impossible with one of those, but there's no telling what desperate people will do. We found him face down, so it's possible he fell on his sword, so to speak.'

'How gruesome,' said Mouse. 'Were you shocked?'

'Not really. It's part of being a policeman,' said George, pink with pleasure at the attention he was receiving.

'What happened to the extra set of daggers?' I asked.

'We've got them down at the station,' he said.

'Will there be an autopsy?'

'Obviously.'

'So, he might not have killed himself.'

'There was a note.'

'But it might be forged.'

'Why can't you ever accept the simple explanation, Tan? The man confessed in writing and then killed himself. Case closed.'

'But what about Felicity Nash?' I asked.

He glared at me.

'Give it a rest. She crashed her car into a tree. There's no definitive proof of sabotage. Ask your pal, Terry.'

His tone warned me not to go on. I shut up, not wanting to provoke him further.

'I'm sure DI Antrim is too busy to speak to me,' I said. 'Well done on clearing up the case. Seacastle is safe again.'

My sarcastic comment hung in the air, but George took it at face value.

'Thanks. I'm off home now, or Helen will send out the St Bernards.'

'Thank you for the takeaway,' said Harry. 'You saved us as well as Seacastle.'

After George had left, I slumped on the couch, feeling defeated. Nothing I had discovered had led me to this conclusion. George's refusal to consider Felicity Nash's death anything other than a tragic accident frustrated me. Harry put his arm around me and squeezed me tight.

'It's Occam's razor, sweetheart. The simplest explanation is most likely the right one, whether you like it or not.'

I pouted.

'It makes little sense. I just don't believe it was him.'

'Or maybe you don't want George to be right?' said Mouse.

'I hate you both,' I said. 'I'm going to bed.'
'Night darling,' said Harry.
'Sore loser,' said Mouse.

Chapter 31

The next morning, I got up early, and after feeding Hades, let myself out of the house, waking no one else. I couldn't face being told to cheer up or to get over it by well-meaning folks. As usual, I had become far too embroiled in the mystery and let it take over my whole life. In the beginning, I wanted to save Grace, but my curiosity had been piqued by the existence of a coven in Seacastle, and deepened by the undercurrents of hate and rivalry I found there. For George and Terry, it was just another case closed, and brownie points all round, but for me it felt personal. And I didn't believe Cyril Wender had killed Dot in an argument over the daggers. It rang falser than my grandpa's teeth.

As I reached the wind shelter, the sun peeped through the clouds and bounced off the rock pools left by the retreating tide. A smell of seaweed and ozone filtered into my nasal passages making me breathe deeply and hold it in before letting it out, slowly trying to clear my mind of resentment. I couldn't expect other people to be as entranced as I was. After all, investigating had been my job for years. It had entered my DNA and changed the way my neurons worked. My pleasure centres reacted to murder and mystery not drugs. The last year had returned me to normal, and now I craved the excitement of the chase. Nothing else would do. But I had to learn to accept defeat too. Nobody wins every time.

Herbert the seagull flew in and cocked his head at me, looking for treats. I threw him some old crusts and bacon rinds, which he snaffled up in an instant before pecking at my pixie boot. I shooed him off and stood up. I needed to clear a space in the shop for Harry to deposit our booty from the cottage and I wanted a catch up with Ghita too. She had been absent for weeks doing a project at the council who now paid her on a consultancy basis. I wanted an update on Surfusion and the state of the boys' relationship. They should have been open months ago, but Kieron's mother never improved enough for him to stay away from her for long. I sometimes wondered if she did it on purpose. Rohan had kept himself busy while Kieron tended to his mother, catering minor events with the help of Ghita. I couldn't help noticing how much calmer he seemed without Kieron's firebrand character riling him up. Rohan and Ghita worked well together and had grown closer with Kieron absent. Ghita's mother had been spot on with her matchmaking; it was just unfortunate for Ghita that Rohan preferred men.

When I got to Second Home, I recced the ground floor to work out how I could fit the new stock in with the old. I had already planned to take the kitchen furniture up to the Vintage to fill in a space beside the window. One of my regular customers had moved into her first property and had bought the 1960s Habitat table and chairs for her dining room.

'I won't be able to afford coffee out for a while with my mortgage,' she said. 'But at least I can drink it at my own piece of the Vintage.'

I busied myself rearranging the furniture downstairs until the doorbell clanged, signalling Ghita's arrival. She carried her large cake tin ahead of her like an offering, which she plonked onto the counter.

'One coffee and pecan for the Vintage,' she said, wiping her brow. Black bags hung under her eyes as I hugged her and her normal happiness quotient had taken a knock.

'Are you okay?' I said, stroking her hair.

Her bottom lip quivered in answer, and I knew we needed to put the kettle on.

'Go up and make us a pot of tea and I'll bring the cake in a minute.'

I watched her climb the stairs with slumped shoulders and steeled myself as I cleared the polish and rags away under the counter. I brought the cake upstairs and put it into the display cabinet with the other edible goodies, extracting a couple of flapjacks for us to eat with our tea. Ghita had made us a pot of builder's tea and set it on the table with a couple of mugs and a small jug of milk. I heard her sniff twice and berated myself for neglecting her. Ghita's demeanour led her to have scores of friends and her fitness classes were full more because of her popularity than their athletic content, but as often happens, her sunny outside hid a raft of insecurities and unspoken hurts which could go unnoticed. I had been so wrapped up in the case, I hadn't realised how desperate she was to download her sorrows.

She gazed out of the window and down the street to the Surfusion restaurant, where Kieron loitered outside, sucking hard on a cigarette. He had arrived back from his sick mother's house after yet another week away, and it looked as if he had had a row already.

'He's back then?' I asked.

Ghita nodded and bit her lip. Her large brown eyes swam with unshed tears.

'What happened?'

'The usual. First, he's all sweetness and light, and then he finds something to complain about. It's always my fault, even when it isn't. Then he turns nasty and…'

Her voice trembled. I wasn't sure how to comfort her. The truth about their virtual ménage-a-trois seemed obvious to me. Kieron suffered from extreme jealousy. Rohan could not speak to another man without Kieron having a tantrum. Their friendship with Ghita had gone well at first. Her talent for devising new recipes and flavours dovetailed with Kieron's flair and Rohan's organisational skills. She adored them and they her. But as time went on, Kieron had become envious of her creativity and her blossoming friendship with Rohan. I had wondered if their partnership would last. What would Ghita do if they broke up? It didn't bear thinking about.

'Maybe you should give them some space? They need time to readjust to each other. Kieron can be a little irrational at times.'

Ghita shrugged.

'Sometimes I wish he'd go to his mother's and never some back,' she said.

'But that would break Rohan's heart and you wouldn't want that would you?'

'No, I guess not.'

She wiped her eyes with a napkin. 'How did I get myself into such a mess? Why can't I fall in love and get married like a normal person?'

'Ah, but you're not normal. You're exceptional. It's hard to find someone to keep up with you. That's why you need two.'

A ghost of a smile hovered on her lips.

'Really? You think I'm exceptional?'

'I know you are.'

Ghita nibbled on a flapjack and I watched her re-inflate as she felt better. I wished I did. I could feel a case hangover lurking, and I couldn't share my woes with anyone. My only hope lay in the skills of Flo Barrington. Nobody could solve the case for her. The evidence spoke to her from the corpse of the victim on her slab, and no other voice could influence her conclusions. No matter what George had decided, Flo went with physical proof alone. Ghita had finished her tea and sat observing me.

'I'm not the only one who's miserable,' she said.

I shook my head. 'Nothing important. They think they found the murderer of Dot Parker-Styles, but I'm sure they haven't. I'm frustrated.'

Ghita frowned.

'They're wrong then, because you are exceptional too and if you think they're mistaken, they probably are.'

I beamed at her. The shop door opened, and I heard Harry's voice.

'Delivery for Ms Bowe.'

We jumped up and went downstairs where Mouse and Harry had already left the first pieces from the van inside the shop. Ghita helped me to take the 1950s kitchen chairs upstairs to the Vintage and to slot the other furniture into the niches I had planned for them. It took us half an hour to unload my items from the van, and then Harry pecked me on the cheek.

'I've got to go to London now, but I'll be back this evening. Don't fret about the case. They couldn't have solved it without your help. You're a star.'

I tried to hide my disappointment.

'You're right. I've got stuff to do here. I don't have time to mope.'

When he had gone, Mouse went to the Co-op to buy milk and sugar for the lunch shift coffees and Ghita headed for the council offices. I couldn't resist phoning Flo. She answered her phone on the first ring.

'I wondered how long it would take you,' she said, laughing. 'I don't need to ask you what you want.'

'Am I wrong to doubt it? Would a man like Cyril Wender kill himself out of remorse and leave a handy note explaining it all in perfect English? It doesn't ring true to me.'

'You think someone murdered him?'

'Isn't that more likely?' I asked.

'I haven't seen the forensics yet. Why don't you leave it with me and stop fretting? I know you.'

'You'll call me if there's any news.'

'I promise.'

Chapter 32

I walked home along the promenade, my head lowered against the wind, which had picked up and whipped the white horses higher. A woman walking two large hairy dogs of indiscriminate breed, whose fur had blown over their eyes, almost trotted past me as the breeze pushed her along the path. She gave me a sympathetic smile as I bent into the wind and headed for home. Upon arriving at my street, I got straight into my car and drove to Sainsbury's to pick up the ingredients for a cottage pie, Harry's favourite. He always returned from London with a raging appetite and we had the same taste in food, which I always rank high in prerequisites for a happy relationship.

The supermarket heaved with people doing their post-work shop, scurrying between the aisles and tutting if the products had been moved to a different shelf. I bought some nice Merlot on a special offer and a bunch of tulips to brighten up the table before queuing up to pay. I had concentrated all day on keeping my thoughts positive and away from Cyril Wender's apparent suicide, but now my mind wandered back to the case. I wondered if the dagger he had used would be one of the original set or a fake. After all, if he could produce almost perfect replicas, maybe even he got confused about which was which. Or witch was witch? Had he known they were precious in more ways than one? I paid and headed for home.

Mouse helped me to unpack the shopping and his eyes lit up as he recognised the ingredients.

'We're having cottage pie? I can't wait.'

'Would you like to make it?'

'Me? But I don't know how.'

'Then it's time you did. Put on an apron.'

'Cool. Can I have the red one?'

I got him to dice the carrots and onions and sauté them in a little butter before adding the beef mince and a stock cube. He mixed the ingredients with great deliberation, the tip of his tongue protruding from his mouth. Then I showed him how much salt and pepper to add.

'Always season lightly. You can put more salt in if it needs some, but you can't take it out, and some people are on low-sodium diets. Oh, and don't forget a dollop of Worcestershire sauce.'

While Mouse supervised the beef filling, I peeled and boiled the potatoes. Then I got him to mash them to the correct consistency to top the pie. His brow wrinkled with concentration as he teased the potato topping over the mince, leaving sharp peaks. I sprinkled a light covering of cheddar shavings on top and then put the pie in the oven.

'Et voila!' I said. 'Your first cottage pie.'

He beamed, then bit his lip.

'Will it taste okay? I don't want Harry to laugh at me.'

'I'm sure it will be delicious.'

We laid the table and then relaxed on the sofa. While we waited for Harry to arrive, I scrolled through my phone enjoying the WhatsApp group we had formed from the remnants of the crew from my former employment on Uncovering the Truth. Since the demise of the show, my colleagues had dispersed all over the industry. Jer Hanlon, a gregarious Irish man who had produced the show, was the live wire in our group. He had moved to a reality show called Sloane Rangers, which had a cast of young people and followed their lives and relationships in gory detail. He always had a morsel of juicy gossip to share with us about the latest goings-on. Mouse loved the show, and he never missed an episode. I pretended to hate it, but secretly I found it fascinating too. Mouse had developed a crush on Daisy Kallis, an obsession he shared with Harry. They both became entranced while she was on screen, making me quite jealous.

Just when I gave up on Harry arriving in time for dinner, he came in whistling and I knew he'd had a good day in London. He kissed me and went to wash his hands in the kitchen, sniffing the air with gusto.

'What's that I smell?' he said. 'Have you cooked me my favourite meal, you wonderful woman?'

'Mouse made it.'

Harry's eyebrows flew up.

'Your talents never cease to amaze me,' he said, slapping Mouse on the back. 'Let's crack open a bottle of vino. I've got news.'

I poured us all a glass of wine and crossed my fingers he had somehow financed a new van. Way off the mark.

'I drove past a sign for Tarton Manor House on the way to London advertising a special offer for a night at the hotel with a 1920s cream tea included. I thought it would be fun to go together, to visit the scene of the crime, so I booked us a spot.'

'Won't the 1920s tea be stale by now?' said Mouse.

'Hilarious. The guests are expected to put on outfits from the era in order to attend the tea. It'll be like a costume party.'

'Am I invited?' said Mouse.

'Not unless you want to share a room with Tanya and me.'

'Yuck, no thanks.'

'Won't it be rather expensive?' I asked.

'Not at all. I got a great price for the furniture in London and I thought you needed a treat after the disappointment of the murder case.'

'You are so sweet,' I said, kissing his bald head. 'I've got great taste in men. One cooks fantastic meals, and the other provides expensive outings.'

'You haven't tasted it yet,' said Mouse.

'Well, if the smell is any sign,' said Harry, 'it's going to be wonderful.'

My phone rang and Flo's number flashed up on the screen. I decided not to answer it and break the mood. I sent her a quick text saying we were about to have supper and she texted me back asking if there would be enough for four.

'Flo's coming to supper,' I said. 'Lay another place at the table please.'

Mouse beamed. He loved Flo. She always treated him like an adult and included him in her conversation, where he hung on her every word.

'The more the merrier,' said Harry.

Flo arrived in minutes, which told me she had been around the corner when she rang us. After she had hugged everyone to within an inch of their lives, we all sat down at the table. I served out portions of Mouse's cottage pie and vegetables and handed them around. Harry tried his first. Mouse watched him for his reaction, his own fork hovering above his food.

'Well?' he said.

'Oh my,' said Harry. 'This is proper grub.'

'You made it?' said Flo. 'It's like the nectar of the gods.'

Mouse blushed to the roots of his hair.

'Really?' he said.

'Scrumptious,' I said. 'You can do all the cooking from now on.'

Harry and Mouse insisted on washing up, so Flo and I sat in the sitting room together drinking tea and enjoying the full feeling that comes from a tasty dinner. I could feel Flo waiting for me, but she broke first.

'You haven't asked me about the autopsy,' she said.

'Should I?'

'Not yet, but I'd like to borrow Mouse tomorrow if I may?'

'Sure. What's it about?'

'Top secret police business. I can't tell you or they'll lock me in a cell on bread and water.'

Flo left soon after, and we had an early night. I tried not to dwell on my disappointment about the murders anymore. In truth, I had zero control over the outcome. I shoved the nagging feeling we had missed something vital to the back of my head and forced myself to sleep.

The next morning, I left for Second Home with Mouse, both of us trying to avoid the subject of Cyril Wender. To be truthful, when Harry had suggested the 1920s tea and a night at Tarton Manor House, I had feigned enthusiasm, even though the idea of going back there did not appeal much. After the disaster of George's wedding to Sharon, I felt as if the place was jinxed. Harry had not picked up on my reluctance, but Mouse had not been fooled. He confronted me about it once we got to Second Home.

'Why don't you want to go to the tea with Harry? It'll be great fun. You should have said something.'

'I know, but our history with the hotel does not inspire me. Harry doesn't associate the place with past failures like I do.'

'Maybe it's time to change that. It's not the hall's fault people used it for nefarious purposes. Anyway, Lydia

Sheldon runs it now. I bet she's changed the atmosphere there. You might even get free champagne. She owes you that much.'

'I'm not sure she's the grateful type, but you're right. I should just enjoy myself and forget the past.'

'What will you wear to the tea?'

'I called Roz this morning. She is lending me a flapper dress owned by her grandmother and Grace has a beaded headband she can lend me.'

'You're going to look fabulous. You should use one of those beaded handbags you hid in the sideboard at home.'

'They're not hidden. They're in storage.'

'They should be in the display cabinet in the shop.'

'They will be.'

He laughed at me. Mouse had become well acquainted with my tendency to hoard items I loved at the Grotty Hovel instead of putting them on sale in the shop. Now and then, he'd pull something out of a cupboard at home and wave it in my face to shame me. The problem with having a vintage shop was the number of fabulous items I wanted to keep.

'Do you mind if I close up early to see Flo at the station on Saturday? She wants me to help her with her computer.'

'Of course not. What's wrong with it?'

'She couldn't explain.'

My turn to laugh.

'What would we do without you?'

Flo had made me promise not to do any further sleuthing until she had confirmed the findings from the autopsy on Cyril Wender. I busied myself in the shop, chatting with customers and serving coffee. I had placed the Alvar Aalto table in my front window and several people had stopped to look at it, including a dealer I had met at the antiques fair. The day flew by. Roz dropped in with the dress, which she made me model for Ghita. They both gushed over the way it hung from my shoulders and over my slim hips. I've always had a slightly masculine figure and this dress could have been tailored for me. I spun around, making the fringe fan out at the bottom.

'Wow,' said Ghita. 'You look fantastic. Harry will melt when he sees you.'

It's amazing how easy it is to feel positive about things when you have people you trust back you. By the time I left work, I found myself looking forward to the weekend instead of presuming it would be an ordeal. I passed by Grace's shop to pick up the headband and found her puzzling over her notes of the case with Max. They had drawn a large complex timeline on a roll of paper to which they had added the key players and suspects.

'What are you two up to?' I said. 'George closed the case.'

Grace arched a thin eyebrow at me.

'George is wrong. And don't act the innocent with me, I know you think so too. Something doesn't fit.'

Max shrugged at me.

'Who am I to disagree?' he said. 'Grace has instincts about this sort of thing.'

I sighed.

'I don't suppose you have spoken to Flo?'

'No. What has she told you?' said Grace.

'Nothing yet, but she's doing the autopsy on Cyril Wender and I know she's not convinced he killed himself.'

Grace jumped up and clapped her hands, her face animated.

'There. Didn't I tell you? I'm good at this?'

'You are, lotus flower,' said Max. 'Why do you think I'm making this timeline with you?'

'Stay here and help us figure this out?' said Grace.

I looked at my watch.

'I'm sorry. I can't stay. Helen's coming over tonight to watch Sloane Rangers with us and I promised to feed her.'

'That programme is stupid,' said Grace. 'We don't like it.'

'It is a little, but Mouse has a crush on one girl, so we watch it anyway.'

'Daisy?' asked Max.

'I thought you didn't watch it?' I said.

'I don't,' said Grace, and glared at Max.

'Good luck with your timeline. Let me know if you find any anomalies.'

Chapter 33

To my surprise, I couldn't wait to go to Tarton Manor House again. Saturday dragged despite my being busy in the shop. But when the dealer returned for my Alvar Aalto table, it seemed as if my day couldn't get any better. Even his dogged bargaining did not deter me. I still made a healthy profit, with which I planned to buy Mouse a new laptop. He took over the reins and shoved me out of the door in plenty of time for me to shower and change. I drove back to the Grotty Hovel where Hades forgot he hated me for an instant and rubbed against my legs. When I bent down to stroke him, he tarried for an instant before dashing off to his basket. I rescued one of the beaded bags from the hall cupboard and took it upstairs, where I transferred my lipstick and money and so on from my handbag.

After a shower, I dried my hair into a bob and put on the headband. I found some green silk pumps in the wardrobe that I couldn't remember buying, but they went perfectly with Roz's dress. I gave a twirl in front of the mirror and liked what I saw. I rarely got dressed up, and I had forgotten how it made me feel liberated and beautiful. Then I went downstairs carrying a small rucksack with some overnight things and waited for Harry. I didn't have to wait for long, and his jaw dropped when I stood up. He gazed at me for several seconds before he could say anything.

'You look amazing,' he said. 'I'm the luckiest man on the planet right now.'

He gave me a tender hug and kissed my neck in a way that made my blood boil. Then he released me again and had another look. He whistled at me, making me blush.

'Come on,' he said. 'I can't wait to show you off at the hotel.'

He looked pretty good himself in a pair of borrowed tails. I felt proud to arrive on his arm and walk up the steps to the hall. A porter took our overnight bags to place in our room and we were directed straight into the tearooms. All around us, people wearing their costumes streamed through into the room, which had a small jazz band playing period music in one corner. We were seated in the opposite corner and could see right across the room. We had a ball commenting on everyone's outfits and admiring the styles. Soon the waiters brought us plates of delicious food; tiny cucumber and mint sandwiches, flaky sausage rolls, smoked salmon rolled with avocado. I took photographs for Mouse and Ghita before tucking in. I could smell the mint from the sandwiches before I tasted it, and the pastry melted on my tongue. Harry gobbled his indiscriminately, but I ate savoury first before launching into the sweet treats.

A cough interrupted my revery. I looked up from my plate to find Lydia Sheldon beaming at me. She had transformed, since I had last seen her, from a bitter old woman into a vibrant woman in the prime of her life. She wore a fabulous golden shimmering shift dress and matching shoes and looked more like an exotic mermaid than the owner of the hotel. I suppressed a snort of disbelief and smiled back at her.

'Tanya? I saw your name on the list yesterday,' said Lydia. 'I thought I recognised it. I owe you an apology and a massive thank you. The police told me you broke the case.'

'The police?' I said, startled George would be so forthcoming.

'A DI Antrim. He was most complimentary.'

'Oh. That was nice. A little surprising.'

'Like your visit. I'm so glad you came,' she said. 'Won't you introduce me to your divine companion?'

Harry leapt to his feet.

'I'm Harry Fletcher. It's a pleasure to meet you. Won't you join us?'

She smiled and sat down.

'And exquisite manners, too,' she said, beckoning the waiter over. 'Can we have a bottle of Moet here please? Bill it to me.'

I tried to protest, but she shook her head.

'It's the least I can do. I've got my life back thanks to you. Look at this place. It's humming.'

She wasn't wrong. The volume of chatter had increased as people relaxed and enjoyed their wonderful teas. The clink of teaspoons on porcelain and the hands reaching for the delicious treats added to the picture of contentment. I could see the pride written all over Lydia's face as she looked around the room. The champagne arrived, and we raised a glass to celebrate the success of her new venture. The bubbles tickled my nose as I took a sip.

'How's business?' I asked. 'Do you have many returning guests?'

'Oh yes. Many couples come here again and again. I suspect some of them are, well, I shouldn't be indiscreet...'

'Lovers? Mistresses?'

'Well, definitely clandestine. There's one couple who've been coming for ages. They disguise themselves in dark glasses and scarves and always arrive and leave separately. They sign themselves in as Ron and Hermione Weasley.'

'They're cheating on Harry Potter?' I said, putting my hand over my mouth in mock horror. 'But that's terrible.'

'It's only a book,' said Harry. 'Let's not get overdramatic.'

'What do they wear?' I asked.

'Not witches' robes, if that's what you're asking. They're always beautifully turned out.'

'Are they booked to come this afternoon?' I asked.

'They're due, but I haven't seen them yet. Maybe they — Oh, wait, there they are now. They're besotted with each other. Aren't they cute?'

They entered the room arm in arm. Hermione gazed at Ron with complete adoration. I almost fell off my chair as it dawned on me who they were. Harry's eyes almost stood out on stalks as he watched them cross the floor.

'Oh, my stars,' he muttered. 'Don't look now, but I think someone's been pulling the wool over our eyes.'

I felt an icy chill run down my back. It seemed as if everything went into slow motion as they walked together to their table.

'This is very important,' I said to Lydia. 'How long have they been coming here?'

'Years, I think. You'll have to ask Tim.'

'Tim Boulting? He's still here?' said Harry.

She shrugged.

'I'm afraid so. I couldn't get rid of him in the end. He's been here for years and knows all the systems.'

I tried not to look horrified at this revelation, but as I was already processing the identity of the Weasleys, my face must have painted a picture.

'Do you know them?' said Lydia. 'I hope I haven't been indiscreet.'

'We are acquainted,' I said. 'But don't worry. They are both single.'

'As far as we know,' said Harry.

'How intriguing,' said Lydia. 'Why all the cloak and dagger?'

'You mean wand and dagger, don't you?' I said.

Lydia laughed.

'I've got to go now. Enjoy your weekend. It's a genuine pleasure to see you back here.'

I waited until Harry signalled she had left hearing distance, and then I moved my chair closer to him. I tried to articulate my shock, but my mouth opened and nothing came out. I gesticulated at them lost for words.

'I know,' said Harry. 'I can hardly believe it myself. What should we do?'

'I'm not sure. Have they seen us?'

'Not yet, but it's only a matter of time. Oh, hang on, they've sat down with their backs to the room. Maybe they're trying to avoid being seen.'

'Let's monitor them and enjoy our tea. They're not going anywhere. I'd like to make sure nobody else joins them.'

'How do we know it's got anything to do with the murders?' said Harry.

'We don't. But maybe we should find out. '

'And how do we do that?'

'I'm not sure, but I have an idea.'

I slipped my phone out of my bag and stood up.

'Give me a minute. Don't eat all the cucumber sandwiches. I'll be back.'

I stepped outside the hall and dialled Mouse's number. He answered on the first ring.

'Why are you calling me? Aren't you having fun? The food looks delicious.'

'There's been a massive break in the case, but I need your help. Are you still fixing Flo's computer?'

'Yes, I am, but—'

'Can you check something for me?'

'On Flo's computer. I don't think—'

'I just need to confirm one thing. Please. You can ask her for permission as long as she keeps it to herself.'

'What thing?'

Chapter 34

I could hardly control my impatience as we ate our afternoon tea and kept an eye on Sir Dudley Seagrove's broad back. Abigail's odd braying laugh broke through the jazz music and floated across the room to us. She often touched Dudley's arm for reassurance as she picked her way through the delicious morsels on offer. Their familiarity with each other spoke volumes about the length of their relationship. They must have been together for years. I found it hard to believe they had anything to do with the tragic deaths of recent times, but they had been hiding their massive secret from us for a reason.

'We've got to speak to them and find out why they lied to us,' I said.

'It should be safe enough here with all these people around. They're not likely to do anything foolish,' said Harry. 'Why don't we bring the champagne over to their table?'

I nodded and stood up. We walked over to them between the noisy tables of people in 1920s outfits. I felt as if I had been transported onto the set of an Agatha Christie movie just before a dramatic scene. My pulse rate rose in anticipation of a showdown and I felt sick. Harry tapped Sir Dudley on the shoulder. He turned around slowly and recoiled in shock as he recognised us.

Abigail's eyes opened wide, and she swallowed. I smiled as if nothing were out of the ordinary.

'Hello, you two,' I said. 'Fancy meeting you here.'

They stared at us in shock. Harry shook Dudley's extended hand. Abigail was the first to recover.

'This is quite the coincidence. We, um, came to this tea together after you introduced us,' she said.

'Did you?' I asked. 'Well, that's odd, because the manager says you've been coming to the hotel together for years as Ron and Hermione.'

'Blast,' said Dudley, avoiding my eyes. 'This is a bit of a pickle.'

'Quite a large one, I'd imagine,' said Harry.

'It's not what you think,' said Abigail. 'Well, it is, but not the dead bodies. We had nothing to do with that.'

'Perhaps we should get a supply of gin-and-tonics and move to the annex,' said Dudley. 'I promise to tell you everything.'

'That sounds like a good idea,' I said.

The two of them stood up, and we followed them out of the room. As the jazz music faded behind us, my mind whirred with explanations for their deception. It had to be connected with the daggers, but I couldn't figure out how. Harry took my hand and gave it a squeeze as Dudley spoke to the waiter and indicated the annex. We walked through the passageway past Tim Boulting's office and into the beautiful conservatory. The silence was almost tomblike after the bustle and music in the tearoom. A waitress fussed over a table for us, setting it out and transferring the delicacies from the tearoom. Then another arrived with a tray containing a bottle of gin, some tonics and bowls of ice and lemon.

'Will that be all, Mr Weasley?' she said, smirking.

'Yes, thank you,' said Dudley.

He shrugged at us, a weak smile on his face. Harry poured four stiff gin-and-tonics and handed them around. I had to add more tonic to mine, but nobody else seemed to notice how strong they were. Dudley flashed Abigail a pleading look. She sighed.

'Where do we start?' she said. 'It's a long story.'

'Why don't you go back to the beginning?' I said.

'I'll do this bit,' said Dudley. 'I think I already told you about Dot and Belinda, my mother, being as thick as thieves. Well, when we were little, they used to sneak off together for meetings at the Cissbury Ring. Abigail spent some time in our house as a result, but I didn't see her often, because my parents sent me to boarding school at seven years old. One summer holiday, we were left to our own devices in my house and we found a box in the attic which contained some weird artefacts. We took them out to play with them, but my mother found us and she made me put them back. She sent Abigail away and told me never to play with them, or her, ever again.'

'I didn't understand why I wasn't allowed to play with Dudley anymore, but I got sent to boarding school at eleven anyway, so we were kept apart by our education,' said Abigail.

Dudley smiled at her and took her hand, which he patted.

'Being forbidden to play with the things I found in the attic only made me more curious, and I snuck up often when I was at home to look at them. Among the things I found up there was a beautiful walnut box which contained a dagger decorated with dragons. There were five empty slots in the box for daggers of the same shape. My mother found me looking at it one night. She did not seem that surprised. Nor did she get angry with me. Instead, we went downstairs to the kitchen where she told me about the Seacastle coven, and how our family had been witches for centuries before, as part of the New Forest coven before our branch separated from them. My great grandmother Agnes had found the daggers among the heirlooms left to us by a certain Brigadier John Seagrove at the end of the nineteenth century. Because of their ebony blades, they are perfect for use as athames in witchcraft. She gave one to each of the families who formed the Seacastle coven to bind us together in magic.'

'We met the Farnhams and the Taylors recently,' I said. 'Each family received one of the original set of daggers, but my friend Grace noticed they were fake.'

'Yes, they contacted me about their daggers after your visit. You put the cat among the pigeons,' said Dudley.

'Was it you who switched the daggers?' said Harry.

'Yes. Since my mother died, I've been switching them out for copies during Wicca ceremonies at Cissbury. It's easy to do in the near dark of candlelight. It's not like anybody would have suspected me of doing it.'

'But why did you take them?' I said.

Dudley shifted in his chair and sighed, but did not answer. Abigail leapt into the breach.

'It was my idea,' said Abigail. 'Our family homes are both in hock because of bad financial management by our parents. When Dudley told me about his ancestor being the original owner of the daggers, I researched them and discovered where they came from. I also found out how much they were worth and I couldn't believe it.'

'I was stunned when she told me. That much money would have solved both of our problems,' said Dudley.

'So, we made a plan to get them back. We contacted a man called Cyril Wender to make us copies of the set, and we substituted the daggers one by one.'

'How did you know about him?' said Harry.

'Oh, Dot used him to fix antiques and create fakes to sell. They were in cahoots.'

'Did Dot know how valuable the original daggers were?' I asked.

'I'm afraid I told her. I should have known she would want to sell them, but then I did not know how much financial trouble she was in,' said Abigail.

'Did you swap hers for a fake one too?'

Abigail shook her head.

'I didn't get the chance. She had hawked the daggers around trying to get the best price. We had no intention of letting her sell them, because she would have gambled the money on the horses, like she'd already done to the house.'

'Is that why you stabbed her?' said Harry.

Abigail turned as white as the tablecloth.

'But I didn't. Why would I kill her? I only needed her dagger.'

'She had planned to sell it to Grace. Maybe you found out and had to stop her?' I said.

She shook her head and turned away. Dudley patted her shoulder.

'Look here,' said Dudley. 'You've got this all wrong. Yes, we paid for a set of fake daggers and swapped them for the real ones. I felt I had a right to the daggers, as family heirlooms, because I would never have been able to persuade the others to give them back. They're so superstitious.'

'Did anyone know about your plan?'

'Not that I know of. We have been very discreet. That's why we've been sneaking around like this. We didn't want anyone to know we were working together.'

'Did Miles know?' I asked.

Abigail smirked.

'Poor dear innocent Miles. He thinks I don't know about the coven. He treats me like I'm still ten years old.'

'But he noticed his dagger was fake.'

Abigail blanched.

'How do you know that?'

'He told the police in front of me. He also visited the other families and noticed their daggers were fake too.'

'Did he suspect us?' said Dudley.

'No. He told me he confronted Dot, and she laughed at him and denied everything. Her dagger had not been switched. He said he was still trying to find out what had happened. When I told him about Dot's car, he thought her death might be connected with the old accident.'

'I don't understand,' said Abigail. 'What has Dot's car got to do with anything?'

I slapped my forehead.

'I can't believe I haven't told you yet.'

'Told me what?'

'Your mother died driving Dot's car. We don't know why she didn't take her own. There is a possibility that somebody sabotaged Dot's car to try and kill her, and your mother died instead. That's why you were thrown clear, as there was no car seat in the back.'

Abigail gasped and grabbed onto Dudley who enfolded her in his plump arms. She sobbed for several minutes before emerging, eyes red and puffy.

'Somebody killed my mother by mistake? But who wanted to kill Dot?'

'We don't know. DI Antrim thought they might have waited until you had grown up before trying again, but there's been a development.'

'What sort of development?' said Dudley.

'Cyril Wender has been found dead beside a suicide note confessing to Dot's murder,' I said.

'So, aren't we in the clear now?' said Abigail.

'It looks that way, but I think they'll find he was murdered. Somebody didn't want him blabbing about the daggers.'

'You mean us?' said Dudley. 'But he did them for us in secret. Nobody knew about them. I paid him a great deal of cash to keep quiet. Why would we kill him?'

'Maybe he tried to blackmail you?' said Harry. 'After all, you just told us he was the only one who knew about the fakes.'

'I hope you're playing devil's advocate here,' said Dudley. 'I don't appreciate being accused of murder.'

'The police will need to talk to you,' I said. 'To eliminate you from their inquiries.'

'We didn't sabotage Dot's car. We were toddlers,' said Abigail.

'I meant for murdering Dot and Cyril,' I said.

'We'll go to the station in the morning and clear all this up,' said Dudley.

'You don't have to wait that long,' said Harry, pointing at the door.

George had entered the conservatory with PC Joe Brennan and another young officer. His grim face told me all I needed to know about his intent. Dudley stood up to face him.

'I'll go quietly,' he said. 'Please don't make a scene.'

'I'm afraid Miss Nash will have to come too,' said George. 'We'll charge you in the station.'

'Charge us?' said Abigail.

'Our forensic consultant completed the autopsy of a certain Cyril Wender today and despite us finding a suicide note at the scene, she believes somebody murdered him. On closer inspection of his accounts, we found a receipt for a set of forged daggers signed by you, Sir Dudley. Since Miss Nash had means and motive to kill her aunt, you are both considered suspects in these cases, which we believe are linked. You'll both have to come with me.'

We watched in stunned silence as Dudley and Abigail got up and left with the police officers. Powerless to do anything, I watched them go. George turned and rolled his eyes at me, but did not direct any comments at us. He stomped off with his 'I'm a detective' stride and disappeared.

'The worst thing is,' I said.

'Worse than this?' said Harry.

'I don't believe they did it, either. We're missing something.'

'Honestly, woman. Finish your drink and let's go to bed. And you are forbidden from mentioning anything to do with the case, or you will sleep on the couch.'

Chapter 35

The next morning, we had breakfast in bed, courtesy of Lydia Sheldon, whose kindness had forced me to revise my opinion of her. I sat in our luxurious four-poster bed, munching flaky chocolate croissants and counting the minutes until we would leave. The chocolate melted on my tongue, giving me a sugar rush. The wonderful view over the grounds from our windows took in the cedar trees and the rolling parkland. I felt guilty for not getting maximum enjoyment from our getaway, but I needed to sit down with Grace and go through our notes. She had been right, not that I doubted her for an instant, but we had missed a vital clue somewhere along the line. Harry tapped my nose with his finger.

'Earth to Miss Bowe,' he said. 'Come in, please.'

'Sorry, sweetheart. I was miles away on another planet.'

'I'm guessing it's Planet Poirot?'

'You know me too well. It should be illegal.'

'So should these croissants. I must have eaten four or five already.'

'Seriously though, darling. I'm so grateful for my treat. I really needed to get away for a few hours.'

'Hm. I'm not sure how well that went after we spotted Abigail and Dudley. We seem to live in a constant maelstrom of suspects and clues right now.'

'Roz says I'm a murder magnet like Jessica Fletcher.'

'Roz is right. Finish your breakfast and give Grace a call. I know you're dying to help her with the timeline. Max is enthusiastic, but he doesn't have the inside knowledge you do. I might take him for a walk on the Downs with Mouse.'

I kissed him softly, tasting the chocolate on his lips.

'Yum. Two of my favourite things. Kissing and chocolate.'

Harry winked at me, and I blushed.

'Maybe we don't need to rush after all,' he said, putting the tray on the bedside table. 'Check out is at midday. Call Grace later.'

Before we left the hotel, I rang Grace, who squeaked with delight when I told her I had big news on the case and needed her help. We met in the Vintage where we could drink lattes and eat cake, while laying the timeline out on a long table. Max offered to come with us, but Harry's suggestion of going for a hike appealed more.

Harry and Max drove off together in my Mini to pick Mouse up at the Grotty Hovel. Grace's eyes shone with excitement as she unrolled the timeline and held it down with a pair of paperweights. They had done a wonderful job of recording incidents and reactions in a clear manner.

'This is fantastic,' I said. 'I've seen nothing like it.'

Grace glowed with pride.

'We used my notes, and the newspaper reports, and information I got from you. Can you add your notes onto the timeline so we can get an overview of the entire case?'

I took my notebook out of my beaded bag, making her laugh.

'Do you take that everywhere?' she said. 'I use my phone to record notes.'

'It's out of habit. Anyway, nobody steals notebooks, only phones. This information is too important to lose.'

I started on the first page of notes and worked my way through the case. Whenever I got to a phrase I had starred, I checked the timeline to see if Grace had put anything down there. We had similar observations about most chats, but nothing that stood out as anomalous. It didn't lead to Cyril Wender either, as far as I was concerned, but nobody else stood out as a key suspect. I went through the timeline again feeling perplexed, and then I made us both a coffee.

'What do we know?' said Grace.

'Dudley and Abigail took back the athames from the coven without telling the other witches, so they paid Jasper Christie, real name Cyril Wender, to make a forged set. They switched out all the daggers, except for Dot's. Miles noticed his dagger had been swapped for a fake and tried to find out who had done it, without alerting anyone to the switch. He confronted Dot who laughed at him. At some stage, Abigail told Dot how much the daggers were worth. That must be when she tried to sell hers to you, but somebody confronted her first and stabbed her with a fake dagger,' I said.

'But what happened to the real dagger? Dot must have had it on her to show to you. Whoever killed her must have taken it.'

'Good point. Nobody seemed surprised when Dot got murdered, but everyone was shocked by the use of an athame. How did they find out about that? It wasn't in the papers?'

'Mrs Farnham said Abigail told them about it. Who else knew?'

'I've got a note here about Perpetua. She told us on our first visit that using an athame for murder was blasphemy and robbed it of its powers. She said it would need to be reconsecrated.'

'But who told her about Dot being murdered with an athame? The only people who knew at the time were the police, us and Abigail.'

I felt a chill run up my spine. Grace stabbed at the timeline with her pen.

'And she hated Dot,' she said. 'She's old enough to have sabotaged the car too. But what was her motive for that?'

'We need to talk to Miles again. He claimed to have known the other witches in the coven all his life. Maybe he knows why Perpetua had it in for Dot? Something that happened in the past, perhaps.'

'It would explain why Perpetua gave up trying to kill Dot after Felicity died instead. And why Abigail thinks someone pulled her out of the burning car.'

'The tattoo! Did you notice if she had one on her arm?' I said.

'We need Miles to help us. Can you call him and see if he'll come over?'

Miles came straight away, alerted by the urgency in my voice. He ran up the stairs of the shop and examined the timeline before he even greeted us.

'I heard about Abigail and Sir Dudley,' he said. 'I've been racking my brains, but I can't think why they would kill anyone. Especially Dot. It makes little sense.'

'We don't believe they did. But they were responsible for the forged daggers.'

Miles gasped.

'I did not know that. I still thought it was Dot who did that. Have you found evidence about someone else?'

'Maybe. We need to ask you some questions.'

'Fire away.'

'You told DI Antrim you knew the sisters from way back. Did you hang around with anyone else?'

'Perpetua Hastings used to be Dot's best friend in those days. They were as thick as thieves.'

A light went on in my head.

'Did they get matching tattoos?'

Astonishment showed on his face.

'How did you know?'

'I didn't until just now. Perpetua seems to hate Dot. What happened between them?'

Miles sighed.

'Roy Loveday. They both hung out with him for months. He had the repute of being a wild man. Girls loved him.'

'He chose Dot though,' said Grace.

'Exactly, before he changed his mind and went on to Flic. Perpetua went into a terrible rage. She said she'd get her own back. I never imagined she would go so far.'

'You knew about the car?'

'No, until you told me, I thought Flic had died in her own car. When Abigail told me about being rescued by someone with a tattoo, I thought she meant Dot. But since you told me about it being Dot's car, I knew it must be Perpetua who rescued Abigail. But it's all so long ago. I didn't see the point of saying anything.'

'Do you suspect her of killing Dot?'

'Not really. She's hardly going to kill her about Roy Loveday twenty years later.'

'What about the daggers?'

'Perpetua's dagger had been switched out. She was livid when I told her that her athame was a forgery. She assumed it must have been Dot, but I told her to wait until I found out the truth. I had planned to confront Cyril Wender and find out who paid him for the forgeries, but then the police got involved. I felt like a prime suspect in that interview. I stayed well out of it in case I incriminated myself somehow.'

'What if she didn't wait?' said Grace.

'That's what I'm thinking,' I said. 'What if Perpetua confronted Dot and killed her in a fit of temper?'

'That means she, or another witch from the Seacastle coven, took the original dagger from the scene and left their forged copy stuck in Dot,' said Grace.

'It's got to be Perpetua,' I said to Miles. 'You have a copy, and so do the Farnhams and the Taylors. Abigail and Dudley now have five originals, but I expect they will have all six when the set is sold to the highest bidder.'

'How do we find out?' said Miles.

'Perpetua said the athames would need to be reconsecrated in a magic circle on the Cissbury Ring. If we invite the six families, we can say we have found the originals, and will swap them back after the consecration. Perpetua will be forced to bring Dot's original with her, or explain how she lost her athame. She won't expect anyone to know hers is Dot's original one. And no matter how carefully she has cleaned it, I'm willing to bet it still has Dot's DNA on it. Possibly even blood if she was holding it when she got stabbed. We can switch it at the ritual and the police can test it for blood and DNA.'

'I can do that,' said Miles. 'I'm sure everyone will come. They'll all be keen to get their original athames back.'

'If you can let us know when and where, I'll make sure George lets Dudley and Abigail out on bail. We can check with Abigail which members of the coven she told about Dot being stabbed with an athame. I'm willing to bet she didn't tell Perpetua. And that puts Perpetua in the frame for Dot's murder. Who else but the murderer would know it was an athame?'

'Abigail and Dudley can bring the second set of forgeries to switch out. It's the magic that counts, rather than the implement. No-one but me will know, and I'm not telling anyone,' said Miles.

'What will happen to the originals?' said Grace.

'I think that depends on Dudley,' I said. 'I expect he'll sell them.'

'Maybe not,' she said, but she didn't elaborate.

Chapter 36

George and Terry needed a certain amount of persuasion to try out our theory about Perpetua Hastings, but in the end, they had no choice but to go with it. They hadn't proved anything against Abigail or Sir Dudley either, and the chance to get solid evidence appealed to both of them. The person who killed Dot had the only original dagger still in circulation, which would be the key to solving the mystery. If Perpetua didn't have it, we'd soon find out who did. The detectives also agreed to let Miles organise meeting the other members of the coven. He had an alibi for the night of Dot's death and had provided the information that led to finding Cyril Wender's body, so he was no longer a suspect. He arranged the meeting for the evening of the full moon a week later.

'We all agreed that the moonlight will cleanse the daggers and help eliminate the blasphemy,' said Miles.

There was no point reminding him that even if we switched the daggers, we would only switch them with the second set of forgeries. The idea of the ceremony had returned his serenity, and he busied himself with organising the best place to hold it. George and Terry would stop the ritual at its height when all the daggers had been placed inside the magic circle and collect them for testing. A sample of DNA would be collected from all the witches to compare against the daggers and the ones used to kill Dot and Cyril. A small crew of uniformed police would be placed in the nearby copse in case back up was required. Grace and I could attend on condition we helped with monitoring the daggers and bagging them as soon as George and Terry stopped the ceremony. Grace was bursting with excitement at being told her role in the sting. Max had to make her a calming cup of camomile to stop her shaking.

Sir Dudley and Abigail had recovered from their ordeal at the police station and were motivated by the prospect of finding Dot's killer and reuniting the last dagger with its peers. Dudley confided to Harry that he had been contacted by a buyer with limitless finances who wanted to take the originals off his hands. I found their glee a little offputting. The entire scheme seemed to me to be sordid and greedy, and while I felt glad that they had not murdered anyone, I was not at all sure I approved of them selling the daggers to the highest bidder. Grace became quite morose when I raised the subject and refused to discuss it with me, but I knew she would have preferred they were returned to Hong Kong, where they belonged.

My anticipation grew as the evening approached. I had experienced nothing similar to the coven's ritual before. The nearest I had got to the supernatural was using a Ouija board in the student dorms at university. We got drunk and scared ourselves silly, but no apparitions sullied our evening. Roz took a dim view of my limited understanding of the process, but she couldn't persuade George to let her come as well. She still harboured resentment about not being able to join the coven for which she felt destined.

'I can't believe you're going to witness the consecration ritual,' she said. 'I'd give my back teeth to come with you.'

'We're trying to catch a murderer,' I said. 'The ceremony is secondary in this case. I'm still not sure where the athame comes in. Why do they need a knife for these events?'

'It's quite simple,' she said. 'The four tools used in Wiccan ritual represent the four elements of earth, air, fire and water. The athame or knife represents fire. It is used for casting of magic circles, controlling of spirits and other ritual purposes. The pentacle symbolises the earth. The circle around a pentagram represents protection and the ever-changing, everlasting circle of life and nature. As an unbroken line, the circle also nods to the ideas of eternity and infinity.'

'Is that why Dot and Perpetua had tattoos of pentagrams on their arms? For protection?'

'I guess so. Wiccans always depict pentagrams point-up rather than point-down. This is because having the point downwards is the Sigil of Baphomet in Satanism.'

'The what?'

'Don't worry about the significance. It's just crucial to ensure your pentagram is positioned correctly or you're sending all the wrong messages.'

'And the other elements?'

'The wand symbolises air and the chalice or goblet water. The chalice is the symbol of the goddess, particularly her womb.'

'And they're all necessary in the ceremony?'

'I've never seen it done, but that's what I've heard.'

The night of the ritual, I dressed in black to make it easier to stay hidden, but Harry told me I looked like a ninja. He and Mouse were being childish about the whole thing, so I tried to ignore them, knowing they were masking their tension with humour.

'I suppose you might be a witch,' said Mouse. 'After all you've got a black cat.'

'He's got a white bib, and he's demonic, so he's the wrong sort of cat.'

'Will you be going on your broom?' said Harry, and they both sniggered.

Then Harry gave me a warm hug and whispered in my ear that I should be careful and he loved me. I felt like staying at home, but I couldn't back out. Shortly afterwards, George picked me up in his car. Terry and Grace were already with him, so we set off for the Cissbury Ring. The skies above Seacastle were clear except for a few stray ribbons of cloud which drifted across the surface of the full moon like coy veils. Grace's face appeared whiter than ever in the moonlight. She sat on the edge of the seat beside me, radiating impatience like a coiled spring ready for action. She had also dressed in black and resembled an avenging pixie. We pulled into the driveway of the church beyond the car park and received last-minute instructions from George about keeping out of sight and how to examine the athames. The whole thing felt surreal to be honest.

We set off through the car park and up the path bathed in moonlight. The crunch of the sandy soil under our feet was the only sound apart from the hooting of a barn owl which floated over our heads like a ghost. Petrichor laden air rose from the damp earth around us. The flashing of a torch alerted us to the hidden uniformed police in the copse to the left of the path way blending with the dark trunks like misshapen trees. We approached the plateau and hid out of sight of the clearing designated by Miles for the ritual. Terry had chosen a patch of thick scrub as a good place for us to wait for the members of the coven to arrive. We squatted or sat on the bank, hidden by the dark fronds of the bushes from anyone approaching, and waited.

'It's a pity we can't take photos,' said Grace. 'It is a once in a lifetime chance to observe this.'

'Phones off,' growled Terry, and I scrabbled for mine in my shoulder bag, panicking in case somebody texted me, giving away our position.

Not long afterwards, the families arrived, dressed in long black robes with hoods. Sir Dudley carried an ancient wooden box. He looked around and stared at the bushes as if he could see us. He knew we were nearby, as George had explained to him he must only bring forged athames to the ceremony. Dudley had not asked why. I think the ghastly series of events around the tragic sisters had knocked the stuffing out of him. He just wanted to be rid of the athames and be back in his house with Abigail. She followed him, her face haggard in the moonlight, and I realised Dot's death had taken a lot out of her. This would be the last straw.

Soon, all eight witches stood on the rise, their robes flapping in the gentle breeze. Miles muttered some incantations and the entire coven joined in the ritual chants, which echoed in the night. Grace pinched my arm, her eyes wide. Then Dudley removed the artefacts from inside the box and placed them on top, making it into an altar. Perpetua took her athame from the sleeve of her robes and drew a magic circle in the dirt around the altar. All the witches stepped inside and Dudley placed a silver pentagram at its centre. Despite my initial scepticism, I found myself drawn into the ceremony by the deep belief of those taking part. I wondered how it felt to stand inside the circle with kindred spirits.

The witches came forward one by one to place the six athames over the pentagram. Miles sprinkled them each with holy water before placing them in a row on the altar. We had all been tasked with watching an athame belonging to one family to make sure we knew whose was whose. Perpetua's athame, which had been assigned to me, was third in line. The witches chanted in an eerie manner, which made the hairs on my arms stand to attention.

'Aradia and Cernunnos deign to bless and to consecrate these knives, that they may obtain necessary virtue through thee for all acts of love and beauty. Aradia and Cernunnos, bless these instruments prepared in thine honour.'

Their faces were etched with what looked like sorrow in the cold light. It felt like the end of an era. George nodded at Terry and he stepped out of the bushes into the moonlight. His tall thin frame threw a devilish shadow over the circle, which made several of the members gasp in shock.

'Hold it right there,' said George. 'I believe one of these athames was the property of Dot Parker-Styles, and was taken from her on the night of her murder. I request that you all wait here with my constables while we check them.'

The police constables appeared from below in the flint mines and herded the witches together like sheepdogs with a flock of black crows.

'This is blasphemy,' said David Taylor. 'You can't do this.'

'I'm afraid I can. I'm sorry about the ceremony, but you will have to perform it another day,' said Terry.

From the rebellious muttering coming from the group, it seemed they were not inclined to accept the interruption. But they did not protest, only whispered among themselves in scandalised tones as PC Brennan placed his frame between them and the circle. We approached the altar with as much reverence as we could muster. It felt odd breaching the circle, like blasphemy. We removed the daggers from the altar one by one. Grace put on a pair of latex gloves and placed a sheet of plastic on a folding table. She picked one up and examined it with a magnifying glass with which was integrated a powerful torch. She peered at the handle and shook her head, replacing the dagger on the altar. An exclamation of relief erupted from David Taylor who was patted on the shoulder by his wife.

Grace followed the procedure with the second athame. Again, she shook her head, and I heard Miles sigh with relief. When Grace got to the third dagger, she paused in her examination and wiped her brow. Then she checked again. This time, she handed the dagger to George.

'This is the one,' she said.

'Are you certain?' said George.

'I'm absolutely sure.'

'Who does it belong to?' said Terry.

'Perpetua Hastings,' I said.

'Ms Hastings, can you please identify yourself?' said Terry, moving over to the group.

'I am she,' she said, throwing her hood back in a dramatic fashion.

The other witches gasped or moved away, leaving her standing in a pool of moonlight, defiance written on her face. George planted himself in front of her and read Perpetua her rights before leaving her in the custody of the constables. They seemed in awe of her until PC Brennan took her arm and propelled her away from the scene. She strode off with them, turning to shout as she left.

'Cowards and fools, the lot of you. I tried to protect us. I did nothing wrong.'

George approached the group and shook Miles's hand.

'Thank you. You can continue with the ritual now if you wish.'

'I think we've had enough of these athames now,' said Miles. 'They are cursed. We will destroy them and find new ones.'

A murmur of assent rose from the others. They stood apart from us, making it obvious we were not welcome any longer. We followed the constables down the hill, trying not to trip as the moon fled behind a bank of cloud obscuring our way. A fine drizzle fell and blanketed the Cissbury Ring behind us.

'Well, that's a first,' said George.

Chapter 37

Once she realised the game was up, Perpetua Hastings confessed everything without preamble and pleaded guilty at her arraignment. She revealed her deep resentment towards Dot's casual attitude which she had interpreted as a betrayal of the coven's secrets and traditions. She claimed that removing Dot had restored the sanctity of the coven and that future generations would see her as a martyr. She had killed Cyril Wender for the blasphemy of copying the sacred athames, which seemed a little harsh, but she did not see it that way. The other members of the coven did not show any inclination to support her. They boycotted her hearing and held a meeting to elect David Taylor as the new head of their group. Sir Dudley and Abigail Nash were ejected without ceremony at the same meeting for their part in the saga, something they did not seem to mind. They moved in together and put Abigail's estate on the market.

But the story didn't end there. No sooner had the kerfuffle over Perpetua's evil deeds died down than the Metropolitan police raided Sir Dudley's house and removed the daggers in their original box before he could sell them. They were acting on a tip off according to George. I did not have to use much imagination to guess who had provided it. I didn't blame her. Grace has strict standards of behaviour which she applies to herself as well as everybody else. I thought she made the right decision. Looting historical treasures from someone else's country is not something I could agree with. Sir Dudley should have given them back himself rather than entertaining offers to buy them.

About a week after Perpetua had been sent to Bronzefield Women's Prison to await trial, we all gathered at the Shanty. George and Terry had offered to buy us a drink as part of the team who solved the case. Harry, Mouse and Max were invited too which went down well. For once, both Ryan and Joy welcomed us into the pub and directed Harry, Mouse, Terry, George, Helen, Flo and me to our favourite corner table. Soon we all had a drink and were passing bags of crisps around. I looked around the group and felt profoundly grateful for my friends as they chatted and laughed. Helen and George radiated happiness which gave me hope they had ironed out their difficulties. Mouse had given up a night with his friends to come with us, and he snuggled close to Flo, reminding me of Hades more than ever. Sometimes I wondered if boy and cat has been reincarnated from a set of twins.

Once we were all settled, Terry held up his hand to silence us and reached inside his pocket taking out some brochures for Bournemouth University. These he handed to Mouse, who examined them as if they were stone age artifacts. He's not used to getting his information on paper.

'I thought you might be interested,' said Terry, ignoring Mouse's obvious bemusement. 'A mate of mine runs the cyber security and digital forensics degree at Bournemouth, and he's agreed to give you a place in September, if you're game.'

Mouse's eyes opened wide and he looked towards me. I swallowed, unsure what to say. I knew we couldn't afford it, but maybe his father could.

'What do you think, George?' I said. 'This sounds tailormade for Mouse.'

'Actually, we've already been discussing it with Flo at the station,' said George. 'There's a bursary going for university study for someone who will work with us after graduation.'

Mouse frowned.

'You mean I have to become a policeman?'

'Not necessarily. You can work as a consultant, like Flo. I'd prefer you came to Brighton, but that will be up to you,' said Terry.

'Can I think about it?' said Mouse.

'Don't take too long,' said Flo. 'The bursary is open for other students to apply if you don't want it.'

Mouse took out his phone and started tapping. George rolled his eyes, but I elbowed him before he could make a barbed comment. The door of the pub opened and Grace and Max came in. We waved them over to the table and Joy brought them a drink. Max raised a glass and toasted the team, but Grace squirmed in her seat as if she needed to go to the bathroom.

'Okay. Spit it out,' I said. 'I'm getting nervous here.'

Max nodded at Grace who reached into her handbag and took out a folded piece of paper.

'Um, well, as you know, Tanya solved the case of Dot Parker-Styles's murder.'

'With a little help from the police,' muttered George.

'And lots of help from you, Grace,' said Terry.

'Thank you. Anyway, when I found out about the true provenance of the daggers, the athames, I approached the Chinese Embassy about them. You may know that Max and I left Hong Kong because of our involvement with the protests. We had to leave most of our things behind and start a new life here in Seacastle. It has been hard for us, because we couldn't risk going back to see our families.'

'Even though we have made lots of nice new friends here,' interjected Max.

Grace tutted.

'Don't interrupt me. As I was saying, I informed the Embassy that I could rescue the daggers for them in return for a guarantee of safe passage to Hong Kong. I spoke to an expert in Antiquities and he negotiated with the government. Anyway, we came to a deal, and they were so happy to get the daggers back, they sent me a large reward which had been offered.'

'Unbeknownst to us,' said Max.

'A substantial reward,' said Grace. 'And so we'd like to give you this check to buy a new van for your business.'

She passed the check to Harry with a small bow. Harry took it and unfolded it. He read the amount and shook his head. I felt tears filling my eyes and glanced at Harry who was struggling to control himself.

'I can't take it, Grace. It's far too much,' he said.

'Oh, but you must, or I will lose face. Without you two, I might be in prison here, or worse, back in China. I hadn't appreciated what wonderful friends I had made here, and how far they would go for me. It's an honour for me to help you.'

'Seriously,' said Max. 'You have to accept it. We need to give it to you or we will be shamed.'

'I don't know how to thank you,' said Harry. 'You've saved our business. I'm so grateful.'

'Mine's a glass of Chardonnay,' said Grace. 'And I need you to help me on Saturday.'

I laughed and poked her in the ribs.

'There's no such thing as a free lunch,' said George. 'I'll have another pint of bitter.'

~~~~~~~~~~~~~~~~~~~~~~~

Thank you for reading my book. Please leave me a review if you enjoyed it.

You can pre-order the next in the series – LAST ORDERS – right here

Other books

The Seacastle Mysteries - a cosy mystery series set on the south coast of England

Deadly Return (Book 1)

Staying away is hard, but returning may prove fatal. Tanya Bowe, a former investigative journalist, is adjusting to life as an impoverished divorcee in the seaside town of Seacastle. She crosses paths with a long-lost schoolmate, Melanie Conrad, during a house clearance to find stock for her vintage shop. The two women renew their friendship, but their reunion takes a tragic turn when Mel is found lifeless at the foot of the stairs in the same house.

While the police are quick to label Mel's death as an accident, Tanya's gut tells her there's more to the story. Driven by her instincts, she embarks on her own investigation, delving into Mel's mysterious past. As she probes deep into the Conrad family's secrets, Tanya uncovers a complex web of lies and blackmail. But the further she digs, the more intricate the puzzle becomes. As Tanya's determination grows, so does the shadow of danger. Each new revelation brings her closer to a chilling truth. Can she unravel the secrets surrounding Mel's demise before the killer strikes again?

Eternal Forest (Book 2)

What if proving a friend's husband innocent of murder implicates her instead?

Tanya Bowe, an ex-investigative journalist, and divorcee, runs a vintage shop in the coastal town of Seacastle. When her old friend, Lexi Burlington-Smythe borrows the office above the shop as a base for the campaign to create a kelp sanctuary off the coast, Tanya is thrilled with the chance to get involved and make some extra money. Tanya soon gets drawn into the high-stake arguments surrounding the campaign, as tempers are frayed, and her friends, Roz and Ghita favour opposing camps. When a celebrity eco warrior is murdered, the evidence implicates Roz's husband Ed, and Tanya finds her loyalties stretched to breaking point as she struggles to discover the true identity of the murderer.

Fatal Tribute (Book 3)

How do you find the murderer, when every act is convincing? Tanya Bowe, an ex-investigative journalist, agrees to interview the contestants of the National Talent Competition for the local newspaper, but finds herself up to her neck in secrets, sabotage and simmering resentment. The tensions increase when her condescending sister comes to stay next door for the duration of the contest.

Several rising stars on the circuit hope to win the competition, but old stager, Lance Emerald, is not going down without a fight. When Lance is found dead in his dressing room, Tanya is determined to find the murderer but complex dynamics between the contestants and fraught family relationships make the mystery harder to solve. Can Tanya uncover the truth before another murder takes centre stage?

Toxic Vows (Book 4)
A shotgun marriage can lead to deadly celebrations
Despite her reservations, Tanya Bowe, ex-investigative journalist and local sleuth, feels obliged to plan and attend the wedding of her ex-husband D.I. George Carter. The atmosphere is less than convivial as underlying tensions bubble to the surface. But when the bride is found dead only hours after the ceremony, the spotlight is firmly turned onto George as the main suspect. A reluctant Tanya is forced to come to George's aid when his rival, D.I. Antrim is determined prove him responsible for her death. She discovers the bride had a lot of dangerous secrets, but so did other guests at the wedding. Did the murderer intend to kill, or has an elaborate plan gone badly wrong?

Last Orders (Book 6)
Has a restaurant critic's scathing review led to his murder?
The grand opening of the Surfusion restaurant attracts a famous food critic, raising the stakes for the owners. The night takes a dark turn when he collapses into his coffee, hours after his scathing review goes live. Local sleuth, Tanya Bowe, a friend of the owners, witnesses the shocking incident and vows to clear their names.

As Tanya digs deeper, what at first seems like an open-and-shut case against the owners unravels into a web of intrigue. Is the famous critic even the intended victim of the crime? Tanya Bowe has her work cut out for her as hidden motives lead to simmering tensions among her friends. With time running out and

Surfusion's future on the line, can Tanya unmask the culprit before it's too late?

Other books by the Author

I write under various pen names in different genres. If you are looking for another mystery, why don't you try **Mortal Mission,** written as Pip Skinner.

Mortal Mission

Will they find life on Mars, or death?

When the science officer for the first crewed mission to Mars dies suddenly, backup Hattie Fredericks gets the coveted place on the crew. But her presence on the Starship provokes suspicion when it coincides with a series of incidents which threaten to derail the mission.

After a near-miss while landing on the planet, the world watches as Hattie and her fellow astronauts struggle to survive. But, worse than the harsh elements on Mars, is their growing realisation that someone, somewhere, is trying to destroy the mission.

When more astronauts die, Hattie doesn't know who to trust. And her only allies are 35 million miles away. As the tension ratchets up, violence and suspicion invade both worlds. If you like science-based sci-fi and a locked-room mystery with a twist, you'll love this book.

The Green Family Saga

Rebel Green – Book 1

Relationships fracture when two families find themselves caught up in the Irish Troubles.

The Green family move to Kilkenny from England in 1969, at the beginning of the conflict in Northern Ireland. They rent a farmhouse on the outskirts of town, and make friends with the O'Connor family next door. Not every member of the family adapts easily to their new life, and their differing approaches lead to misunderstandings and friction. Despite this, the bonds between the family members deepen with time.

Perturbed by the worsening violence in the North threatening to invade their lives, the children make a pact never to let the troubles come between them. But promises can be broken, with tragic consequences for everyone.

Africa Green – Book 2

Will a white chimp save its rescuers or get them killed?

Journalist Isabella Green travels to Sierra Leone, a country emerging from civil war, to write an article about a chimp sanctuary. Animals that need saving are her obsession, and she can't resist getting involved with the project, which is on the verge of bankruptcy. She forms a bond with local boy, Ten, and army veteran, Pete, to try and save it. When they rescue a rare white chimp from a village frequented by a dangerous rebel splinter group, the resulting media interest could save the sanctuary. But the rebel group have not signed the cease fire. They believe the voodoo power of the white chimp protects them from bullets, and they are determined to take it back so they can storm the capital. When Pete and Ten go missing, only Isabella stands in the rebels' way. Her love for the chimps unlocks the fighting spirit within her. Can she save the sanctuary or will she die trying?

Fighting Green – Book 3

Liz Green is desperate for a change. The Dot-Com boom is raging in the City of London, and she feels exhausted and out of her depth. Added to that, her long-term boyfriend, Sean O'Connor, is drinking too much and shows signs of going off the rails. Determined to start anew, Liz abandons both Sean and her job, and buys a near-derelict house in Ireland to renovate.

She moves to Thomastown where she renews old ties and makes new ones, including two lawyers who become rivals for her affection. When Sean's attempt to win her back goes disastrously wrong, Liz finishes with him for good. Finding herself almost penniless, and forced to seek new ways to survive, Liz is torn between making a fresh start and going back to her old loves.

Can Liz make a go of her new life, or will her past become her future?

The Sam Harris Series (written as PJ Skinner)

Set in the late 1980's and through the 1990's, the thrilling Sam Harris Adventure series navigates through the career of a female geologist. Themes such as women working in formerly male domains, and what constitutes a normal existence, are developed in the context of Sam's constant ability to find herself in the middle of an adventure or mystery. Sam's home life provides a contrast to her adventures and feeds her need to escape. Her attachment to an unfaithful boyfriend is the thread running through her romantic life, and her attempts to break free of it provide another side to her character.

Fool's Gold - Book 1

Newly qualified geologist Sam Harris is a woman in a man's world - overlooked, underpaid but resilient and passionate. Desperate for her first job, and nursing a broken heart, she accepts an offer from notorious entrepreneur Mike Morton, to search for gold deposits in the remote rainforests of Sierramar. With the help of nutty local heiress, Gloria Sanchez, she soon settles into life in Calderon, the capital. But when she accidentally uncovers a long-lost clue to a treasure buried deep within the jungle, her journey really begins. Teaming up with geologist Wilson Ortega, historian Alfredo Vargas and the mysterious Don Moises, they venture through the jungle, where she lurches between excitement and insecurity. Yet there is a far graver threat looming; Mike and Gloria discover that one of the members of the expedition is plotting to seize the fortune for himself and is willing to do anything to get it. Can Sam survive and find the treasure or will her first adventure be her last?

Hitler's Finger - Book 2

The second book in the Sam Harris Series sees the return of our heroine Sam Harris to Sierramar to help her friend Gloria track down her boyfriend, the historian, Alfredo Vargas. Geologist Sam Harris loves getting her hands dirty. So, when she learns that her friend Alfredo has gone missing in Sierramar, she gives her personal life some much needed space and hops on the next plane. But she never expected to be following the trail of a devious Nazi plot nearly 50 years after World War II … Deep in a remote mountain settlement, Sam must uncover the village's dark history. If she fails to reach her friend in time, the Nazi survivors will ensure Alfredo's permanent silence. Can Sam blow the lid on the conspiracy before the Third Reich makes a devastating

The Star of Simbako - Book 3

A fabled diamond, a jealous voodoo priestess, disturbing cultural practices. What could possibly go wrong? The third book in the Sam Harris Series sees Sam Harris on her first contract to West Africa to Simbako, a land of tribal kingdoms and voodoo. Nursing a broken heart, Sam Harris goes to Simbako to work in the diamond fields of Fona. She is soon involved with a cast of characters who are starring in their own soap opera, a dangerous mix of superstition, cultural practices, and ignorance (mostly her own). Add a love triangle and a jealous woman who wants her dead and Sam is in trouble again. Where is the Star of Simbako? Is Sam going to survive the chaos?

<u>The Pink Elephants - Book 4</u>

Sam gets a call in the middle of the night that takes her to the Masaibu project in Lumbono, Africa. The project is collapsing under the weight of corruption and chicanery engendered by management, both in country and back on the main company board. Sam has to navigate murky waters to get it back on course, not helped by interference from people who want her to fail. When poachers invade the elephant sanctuary next door, her problems multiply. Can Sam protect the elephants and save the project or will she have to choose?

<u>The Bonita Protocol - Book 5</u>

An erratic boss. Suspicious results. Stock market shenanigans. Can Sam Harris expose the scam before they silence her? It's 1996. Geologist Sam Harris has been around the block, but she's prone to nostalgia, so she snatches the chance to work in Sierramar, her old stomping ground. But she never expected to be working for a company that is breaking all the rules. When the analysis results from drill samples are suspiciously high, Sam makes a decision that puts her life in peril. Can she blow the lid on the conspiracy before they shut her up for good?

Digging Deeper - Book 6

A feisty geologist working in the diamond fields of West Africa is kidnapped by rebels. Can she survive the ordeal or will this adventure be her last? It's 1998. Geologist Sam Harris is desperate for money so she takes a job in a tinpot mining company working in war-torn Tamazia. But she never expected to be kidnapped by blood thirsty rebels.

Working in Gemsite was never going to be easy with its culture of misogyny and corruption. Her boss, the notorious Adrian Black is engaged in a game of cat and mouse with the government over taxation. Just when Sam makes a breakthrough, the camp is overrun by rebels and Sam is taken captive. Will anyone bother to rescue her, and will she still be alive if they do?

Concrete Jungle - Book 7 (series end)

Armed with an MBA, Sam Harris is storming the City - But has she swapped one jungle for another?

Forging a new career was never going to be easy, and Sam discovers she has not escaped from the culture of misogyny and corruption that blighted her field career.

When her past is revealed, she finally achieves the acceptance she has always craved, but being one of the boys is not the panacea she expected. The death of a new friend presents her with the stark choice of compromising her principals to keep her new position, or exposing the truth behind the façade. Will she finally get what she wants or was it all a mirage?

Box Sets

Sam Harris Adventure Box Set Book 2-4
Sam Harris Adventure Box Set Book 5-7
Sam Harris Adventure Box Set Books 2-7

About the Author

I write under several pen names and in various genres: PJ Skinner (Travel Adventures and Cozy/Cosy Mystery), Pip Skinner (Sci-Fi), Kate Foley (Irish contemporary), and Jessica Parkin (children's illustrated books).

I moved to the south coast of England just before the Covid pandemic and after finishing my trilogy, The Green Family Saga, I planned the Seacastle Mysteries. I have always been a massive fan of crime and mystery and I guess it was inevitable I would turn my hand to a mystery series eventually.

Before I wrote novels, I spent 30 years working as an exploration geologist, managing remote sites and doing due diligence of projects in over thirty countries. During this time, I collected the tall tales and real-life experiences which inspired the Sam Harris Adventure Series, chronicling the adventures of a female geologist as a pioneer in a hitherto exclusively male world.

I worked in many countries in South America and Africa in remote, strange, and often dangerous places, and loved every minute, despite encountering my fair share of misogyny and other perils. The Sam Harris Adventure Series is for lovers of intelligent adventure thrillers happening just before the time of mobile phones and the internet. It has a unique viewpoint provided by Sam, a female interloper in a male world, as she struggles with alien cultures and failed relationships.

My childhood in Ireland inspired me to write the Green Family Saga, which follows the fortunes of an

English family who move to Ireland just before the start of the troubles.

I have also written a mystery on Mars, inspired by my fascination with all things celestial. It is a science-based murder mystery, think The Martian with fewer potatoes and more bodies.

~~~~~~~~~~~~~~~~~~~~~~~~~~~~~~~~~~~~

Follow me on Amazon to get informed of my new releases. Just put PJ Skinner into the search box on Amazon and then click on the follow button on my author page.

Please subscribe to my Seacastle Mysteries <u>Newsletter</u> for updates and offers by using this QR code

You can also use the QR code below to get to my website for updates and to buy paperbacks direct from me.

You can also follow me on <u>Twitter</u>, Instagram, Tiktok, or on <u>Facebook</u> @pjskinnerauthor